The Die Decides
CM Lowry

This book is dedicated to my incredible wife Katherine. Thank you, for all you do, and for everything you are.

Also, I dedicate it to the noisy gaggle of children who make our lives utterly exhausting, and all the richer for it.

Finally, for my silly friend Dave, who truly understands the beautiful, burdensome gift that creativity can be.

Published in 2022 by Beyond Cataclysm Books.

First edition January 2022
Design, Layout and Typesetting by C.M. Lowry
Illustrations by C.M. Lowry, Dave Emmerson, Toby Prest, Gaelen Adric Izatt-Galloway III, Dickkie Watson, Wiley Murder Willis and Joen Lowry.

ISBN 978-1-914260-02-5 (hardback)
ISBN 978-1-914260-03-2 (ebook)
www.allaboutchris.org

Published under non exclusive license by

beyond
cataclysm
books

Beyond Cataclysm Books
42 Mersey Walk
Warrington, United Kingdom
WA4 1SY
www.beyondcataclysm.co.uk

Contents

Introduction

It was easy to fall in love with microfiction.

Bite-sized adventures are fun for everyone, and wrapping stories into impossibly tiny spaces is a delicious challenge for writers.

The book you are holding was funded by my generous backers - thank you! - and the composition and length of each story chosen by a single ten sided die. I talk about some of the challenges and joys of this at the end of the book.

Unfortunately, I allowed the Die to decide how long this introduction could be: it only gave me 100 words. It appears that it wanted you to start enjoying the stories instead...

Arna tucked a loose spoon under the table's elastic straps. The silverware was battered and tarnished. Frankly, at best it was silver*ish*ware. Some of it was shiny. In patches.

The spoon stayed in place, but jiggled in protest against its rubber prison.

It was too hot in the dining cabin, and yet - unfairly - also suffered from flashes of chilling breeze. Nothing could be done about either problem. Housed directly beneath the engine room, the cabin shared an entire wall with the steam tanks. "Too hot" was unavoidable. And breezes? Well, you try nailing together planks for walls without leaving gaps. Even a few rooms deep, the wind finds its way through - especially with an altimeter reading "19 thousand feet" and engine controls dialled to "go like the clappers".

Arna continued clipping steel dishes in place, one by one. Each made a scratchy 'clunk' as it caught in place, held by magnets in the wood.

Tom noticed that visibility had improved, as he peered through the windscreen. The ice storm had cleared the air. There had been one point earlier where they may well have been underwater, for all he could make out through the tapestry of hail, condensation and frost. Presently he could see for miles, with tufts of altocumulus clouds forming a carpet of giant castles and undulations from horizon to horizon.

The sun was nearly set, everything glowing in a fashion that seemed somehow brighter than reality. And colder. For all the sun and clear skies, the air was somehow cooler than when the ship was clasped in the frozen cirrus fury of the ice squall.

He shivered, and considered putting on another scarf; suddenly a bell rang out deep below.

Thoughts of scarves were put aside. He could cope for another five minutes - it was nearly time to eat!

The brass rim of the bell vibrated, shimmering between real and unreal. Cook paid no attention to it. Everything was coming together in the usual flurry. Excitement about ringing the dinner call had worn thin twenty years ago; it was now just a reminder that washing up was looming.

She wiped her hands on a grubby apron and spun round to the next pan. It was slopping in approximately the right consistency, so she moved it off the steam vent, and brought the stinns back on for a final warm through. A stringy sort of vegetable, with bits that caught between your teeth; but they were cheap, and available by the bucket-load at the last port. Complain though the crew might, a ladle of boiled stinns was less unpleasant than developing scurvy. Better bits in your teeth than *missing* teeth, right?

Behind her, the bell continued to blur as the energy within it faded away. She bustled. It was nearly time, and still more to be done.

From a distance, the Hereward hung from its balloon, completely isolated. The peach skies were otherwise empty, the airship a single tiny speck in a lonely expanse.

From a closer vantage, however, one might make out a tiny figure, stood improbably atop the giant air bag itself. One might wonder why the figure held its arms out so wide and high, when an inevitably fatal fall awaited the smallest of mistakes.

Mouse hopped between seams, bouncing on their heels and using the buoyancy of the canvas to spring a little higher with each jump. It almost felt like flying. In a way, it *was* flying, except that if the ship disappeared, the rest of the flight would be very much in a "down" direction.

The dinner bell rang out, its normally sonorous tones weedy in the high air. Mouse made their way to the ladder, doing a cartwheel as they did so, briefly enjoying an upside down sky.

Stomachs stirred as Cook clonked the pans down. A succulent smell filled the humid air.

"Stew! What we got with it?", Mouse asked, still breathless. "Any bread?"

"Something satisfying and healthy", said Cook emphatically.

Mouse visibly deflated and Arna groaned, "Stinns? Again?!".

Captain Tom glared at them both, "Finished being rude, you two?".

He nodded at Cook, and she lifted the tarnished pan lid with a flourish. "Dinner is served!"

THE GRAND SERVICE

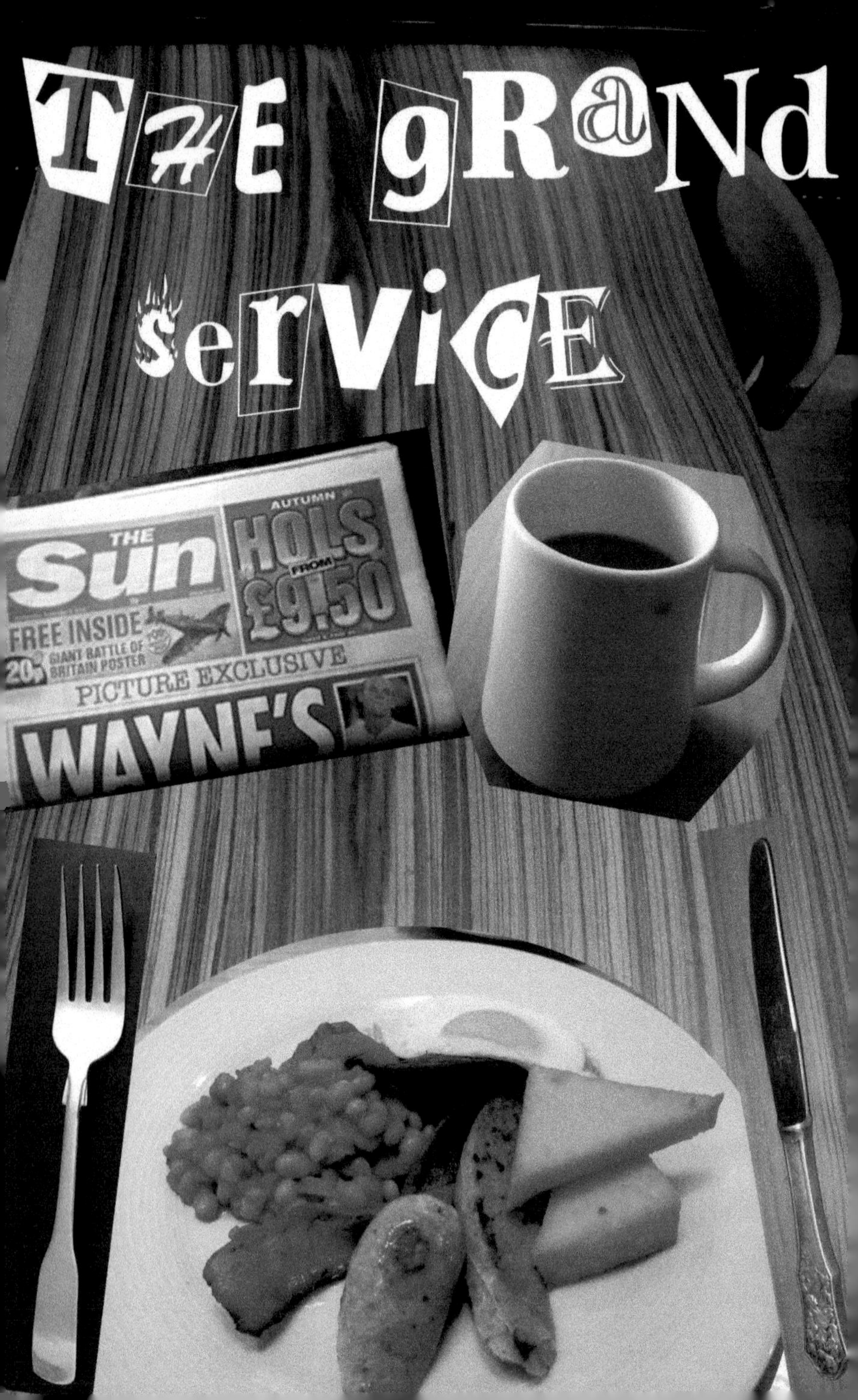

The Grand Service

900 crime dinnertime

I laid my copy of The Sun out on the table - after clearing a space amongst the clutter of ketchup bottles and cutlery. I pointed to the little picture on page 9. "Dave! Look at this".

He squinted at it, "What is it? Some kinda shield?"

I rolled my eyes at him. "No, not a shield. It's a plate. One of the Queen's own plates, in fact."

Dave squinted at it. "Looks like a shield to me". He went back to chewing an over-fried sausage.

Leaning back in my chair, I read the rest of the article with increasing interest. You've heard of 'The Crown Jewels', right? Big old shiny things, locked up in London Bridge with a million guards? Only a moron would try to nick them.

Bet you ain't heard of 'The Grand Service' though? Turns out, back in 18-whenever, King George paid a pretty penny for enough gold-plated crockery to serve his entire inbred family at once. It became known as *The Grand Service*; 288 plates, each one a work of mastery, majesty and no detectable trace of modesty.

Of course, such a treasure is far too nice to use every day; it's only wheeled out on special occasions. One of which was coming up next month, according to the paper. A state banquet, with the Queen and other European bigwigs, at St. James Palace.

Such an occasion presents opportunities for individuals of enterprise, I considered, as I wiped up the remains of my egg with a piece of half-fried half-burnt bread.

Two weeks later, and the plan was in action. Dave was in the van, obviously. Not exactly the sharpest spoon in the drawer, and I didn't think he'd be an asset bluffing access to a *bona fide* Royal Residence.

We had a two pronged strategy. Posh Arnold had joined the ranks of "Bespoke Food" - the caterers at the reception. It had to be him because a) he's posh, so he'd fit in, and b) he's the only one with an even slightly clean criminal record.

They'd already had him waiting at three events, so predictably he'd been complaining about having to do some actual work for once. Moaning aside, he'd confirmed that there were a large number of new, temporary staff, enough that unfamiliar faces wouldn't be noticed.

I was responsible for the rest of us. It took literally 2 minutes on Google to confirm that the palaces use external providers to manage their electricity supply. With this information in hand, I entered Palace's postcode into an energy switcher and requested a change of provider. This triggered an automated letter to be sent to the address. I allowed a few days for the post to arrive, and then called the St James Director's Office - the direct number being available on their website, naturally.

"Hello! Mr Simons from UK Power Networks here. Please may I speak to Mr Manifold, your head of infrastructure?"

Always provide the name of someone you are expecting to speak with. It puts receptionists on the back foot, like they are the ones in the wrong.

"Oh... I don't know Mr Manifold... Do you mean Ms Williams, she usually deals with utilities...?"

See what I mean? "Ah yes, Ms Williams, thank you."

Within minutes I'd apologised for the automated letter - my knowledge of its existence providing ample evidence that I worked for UK Power - and arranged a routine services check on the morning of the reception.

Ms Williams herself met us at the Marlborough Road side gate. She glanced at our UK Power lanyards and jackets - £23 from the print shop on Wanstead High Street - and took us down the corridor to a utility room. It was all painted pipes and brass plaques, very 1960s. "The main meters are here, although I'm sure there are others..." She waved vaguely, with precisely the lack of expertise I was hoping for.

"Ah, yes, we'll check this area, and search out any others following the ducts", I said, wielding a technical-looking gadget I'd bought at Poundland the day before. It was actually only useful for checking the temperature of roast chicken, but Ms Williams appeared unaware of this.

"Well, if that's all you need me for, I'll leave you to it", said Ms Williams, "There's a very important event upstairs, so please stay on this floor..."

After she left, it took us moments to change into the catering outfits hidden in our tool bags. The back stairs led us directly up to the kitchens, where our "Bespoke Food" lanyards passed a bored security officer's extremely cursory inspection.

After that, it was just a matter of timing, each of us leaving the dining hall holding two plates yet mysteriously reaching the kitchen with only one. A remarkably incident-free exit followed - even despite the set of 19th century silverware we each had tucked into our underpants.

Back in the utility room, we all changed back into hi-vis, and walked calmly out to the van. Our passage went unquestioned.

Dave had just started the engine... when Ms Williams came running out.

She shouted, "Mr Simons, stop!"

"Calm, boys!", I whispered tersely, holding out a hand.

She rushed up to the van. "You forgot this!", she said, and deposited the chicken thermometer into my hands.

All I could trust myself to say was, "Thank you".

Ms Williams smiled, and turned to the guard, "Open the gates please".

She even waved as we drove away!

Galactic Fade Engineering
Authority

Operating
Instructions
Series AB-96 Rayship

01 Document 011.   //500 //scifi //mastery

01 Document OI1

Operating Instructions for Series AB-96 Rayships

02 Warning: Ray diving is a dangerous activity. It can represent a threat to life, ship and stellar continuity. It should only be undertaken by qualified and registered pilots, in specific incidences sanctioned by the relevant Galactic Fade Engineering Authority (G.F.E.A.).

Unsanctioned raydiving is a <u>RED LEVEL</u> Treason Offence in all regions of the Unified Territories - punishable with decommission; ie. death for organic lifeforms, and reformatting for AI based sentients!!

03 Initialisation: It should not need to be stated, and yet multiple incidents have occurred in recent decants, so we shall be explicit: space suits must be worn when diving into a star.

Obviously. Even a 'cool' star has temps exceeding 2500°K. Relying on a handheld statis field is idiotic.

As your parent doubtless told you:
Suit up or melt up!

04 Minimum Velocities: Again, it is disappointing to need to remind trained professionals, but the supernova incident at Key-Alpha-06 highlights the disregard that some pilots still take to this: dives must be completed as quickly as safety permits.

You do not want to be "hanging around" inside a star. Get in, get out. Your job is to identify Fade deposits suitable for utilisation – you are _not_ there for a holiday. Stopping to broadcast a selfscreen to your mates is not appropriate, and could lead to starcore destabilisation. And your death.

05 Maximum Velocities: Please also take care to restrict yourself to appropriate maximum speeds. Please refer to document OI1ST for the cross-linked table which clearly lists safe maximums based on stellar mass, size and proximity of galactic neighbours.

Yes, it is possible to go faster than the recommended velocities, and yes, most of the time you won't have any problems. But the increasing prevalence of cosmic trails following high velocity dives has been noted by the G.F.E.A.

The actions by a small-but-growing group of pilots to intentionally shape exit routes is also strictly forbidden! Depositing cosmic matter in planned patterns and shapes is unprofessional, and the action of one ship to leave the message "ARKON SUCKS" permanently glowing in the skies of Arkon-7 is still under investigation.

Penalties <u>will be paid</u>, so please don't do it! Even if it seems really funny at the time.

06 Soiling Fade Deposits: Finally, Fade deposits, when discovered, should be documented but left alone. No interference should be made in their composition.

Look, we know you are in the middle of a star, and it shouldn't matter, but ejecting ship waste daring dives is *entirely* unsanctioned. It won't "just burn up", as the defendant in a recent Tribunal stated. Fade deposits are n-dimensional entities that treat time and temperature very differently from normal space.

And well, there's no nice way to say it — they aren't convenient toilet disposal sites. No one wants to engage a Fade miner only to have the intakes clogged with transdimensional bog roll. Or worse.

You know who you are, so please stop it!

08 Thank you for reading. If the above is not clear, please contact your local G.F.E.A. for guidance.

Remember — be safe, be considerate, please try not to blow up any planets.

G.F.E.A.
Administration

Elsa Mi'Fbir
Fade Deposit Inspector

You push your head through the turquoise hanging beads. There's no one inside, so you duck through the doorway, and stand. There are several chairs there, tucked in round a little table. Might be okay to sit down, you aren't sure, so you hover, awkwardly.

Just as you start to wonder about calling out, or looking for a bell to ring, the inner door opens. A lady walks through. She has dark green hair in a dense sweep, half hiding her face. "They will call you through soon". No eye contact. Before you can think of any sort of response, or even if one is necessary, she leaves. The door closes.

There are no magazines, no books, no TV. Aside from the table and chairs, the only furniture in the room is a tall wooden floor lamp with a flickering filament. After staring at it for a few seconds you have to look away; it might set off your migraines.

You sit. Time passes. Your eyes are drawn back to the stuttering light. You begin to wonder if this was a bad idea.

A rattling from the door draws you back to alertness. You hear muffled words. The door handle shakes. Then, a man appears, half falling into the room. He looks amused rather than embarrassed, "Sorry, thought it was locked". His hair is dark green. Is his skin slightly tinged too?

He steps in, lightly, barely touching the floor, and sits at the table opposite you. There is definite eye contact, and it's sudden and intense. You've never seen eyes as green, nor as bright. And constant. They somehow mock the room's feeble light source. Challenge it.

"Greetings!" Hands wide. As wide as his grin. "Now is the moment. Sure you want to do this?"

Well, are you?

CENTRAL TERRITORY

STATE
INTEGRATED
LIVING
OBELISKS

ORDER & EFFICIENCY

Silos passed beneath us. Each was perfectly circular and equally spaced from its neighbours. They went on forever, like a field of infinite bowling pins. All waiting for a big old ball to come crashing through.

I appreciated the clear arspex in the floor of the cop car. It gave me something to look at, as they transported me to the law plaza. Hard to look at much else, face down with your arms secured behind you and an officer's boots holding you flat.

From this high, you couldn't see people, just the splashes of green between each huge building. I think your average silo holds 10,000 people? Something like that anyway. Here in Central territory the state likes things in neat lines, and they like civs to stay within those neat lines.

Hence the rows and rows of identical State Integrated Living Obelisks. I'm sure some committee chose that final word to make them sound historic, magnificent. *Obelisks*. "These aren't huge cattle sheds, no, these are *art*". Of course, that lasted about a minute, and then everyone shortened it to S.I.L.O. They even look like the old grain silos, except it's all us piled up inside them instead of wheat.

The rows of silos were briefly interrupted by a river, and then carried on. An endless, populated monotony with nature just getting in the way

Silos are incredibly efficient. Self-powered with solar and geothermal energy, they have schools, homes, shops, hospitals, libraries. They are self-contained, with everything a growing civ needs; birth, life, work, death, and anything in between. Except self-expression. Identity.

Finally, the structures came to an end. There was the narrow strip of the Central Parks before the squat uniformity of the Administrative Quarter began.

Let me tell you about parks, for a minute. Back in the early 20th Century, some plucky citizens of a territory called "England" made a stand. Back then, there were huge areas of wild, rugged country owned by rich people. General members of the populace were not allowed onto these privately owned hills and mountains. After some tussles back and forth, the situation culminated in hundreds of civs climbing a mountain together to say, symbolically, that the wilderness has no owner.

Central territory found a solution to that. They left us no wilderness.

I tilted my head, crushed as it was against the arspex, straining to look as far as I could in every direction. Left, right, north, south. And yet, all I could see was the trim lines of endless silos. To the horizon and beyond. Nothing of the wild remains - even the mountains have been flattened.

Why have an outside world when you can throw on a headset and be transported anywhere the designers want you to go. Well, anywhere the state allows the designers to want you to go.

The car was dropping lower now. I started to make out details; people, windows, faces. They might as well have been blank. Barely any different to the tex of the everlasting silo walls.

No one thinks to stand on forbidden rocks any more. Most of the time it feels like I'm the only individual in the world. Everyone else is just a drone.

The pressure on my backplate lifted. A jolt ran through my torso; the guard had used his baton on me. I would have reminded him that I was a civ, just like them, but he wouldn't have cared. A warning flashed in my vision; my CPU had not enjoyed that high voltage fluctuation.

I trailed behind the cops across the plat. Even at this time of day there was a hubbub of off-duty police, recently paroled civs and the hidden-in-plain-sight scramble of droids doing the dirty work, from cleaning vents to physically restraining perps.

One vending bot caught my eye. Its right-sided service arm was broken, hanging off at an angle. There was a level of desperation there, as it tried to jolly passers-by into buying a burrito.

In a world of human-made perfection, where nothing of nature has been left untainted, how ridiculous is it that we, the robots, humanity's finest creation, are always inches away from obsolescence?

We arrived at the booking desk. Through the whispnet, I engaged with the check-in AI; Crime? it asked.

Civil disobedience, I transmitted. Not sorry, and there was no use denying it.

Reason?, the main camera turning to study my own scratched countenance.

I looked over at the vendbot once more, one-handedly trying to put a hot dog together. A boy was laughing.

Reason?, the AI repeated in exactly the same tone.

I looked into the camera, at the supervisor viewing me from a mile away, and I told them why. If the wilderness has no owner, neither have I.

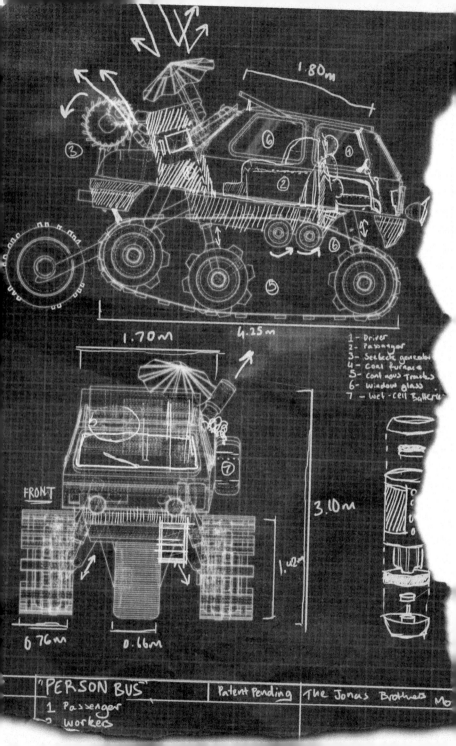

1.80m

③

6

①

2

6

5

1.70m   4.25m

1 - Driver
2 - Passenger
3 - Seebeck generator
4 - Coal furnace
5 - Continuous tracks
6 - Window glass
7 - Wet-cell Batteries

7

FRONT

3.10m

1.42m

0.76m   0.66m

"PERSON BUS"   Patent Pending   The Jonas Brothers MJ
1 Passenger
→ 2 Workers

Eminently experimental
900 coalpunk green leaves

Rain hammered against the steel chimney. Esau ducked under the protruding rebar, and felt the roof for leaks. Bone dry. He let out a fierce grin, surprising himself. Nice to have something go right for a change.

He banged a hand against the burnished wall. The whole personbus resonated. "Let's get going, Frankie!", he yelled.

An answering shout called out, and a grinding noise began below, as the Seebeck generator switched on, and the articulated tracks began to pull them forwards. A brass plate vibrated, until the lettering - "The Jones Brothers Motorating Personbus (Patent Pending)" - blurred.

Esau carefully centred his cap and peered out at the road in front. The rain made it hard to see; there were rivers pouring down the glass in front of him. The windowglass was a fantastic innovation; it beat facing winter gales head-on with a cap and goggles as your only protection. However, when the weather got particularly wet visibility could drop dangerously low. Perhaps the solution would be some kind of permanent umbrella in front? The idea needed more work.

Even with the rain, the steady cobbles of King's Street were obvious - to the eye *and* the buttocks. The suspension on the personbus was currently *experimental* - Frankie's terminology for *"broken and unlikely to be fixed any time soon"*. The plus side of continuous tracks is that they can easily travel the muddiest of unpaved roads - and Manchester in February has little shortage of those. The downside is they make cobbles even more uncomfortable than wheels do.

They rattled along the street, a great cloud of coal smoke and steam billowing behind them. The rain was colliding with the billowing vapour, condensing and falling to the ground as dirty grey water.

Over the next thirty minutes, they left the built-up town behind them, heading south and east. Three storey town houses were replaced with warehouses, off Chester Road, and then these too faded away. Their passenger, a Ms Larton, who lived on "private means", lived farther still, in the quiet rurality between Stretford and the upstart terraces of Moss Side.

They pulled, eventually, onto Seymour Grove, and Ms Larton's dwellings. In truth, she was more than a passenger; Ms Larton was their patron, and an indulgent one at that. More than once Esau had gone to her, shamefaced, after another setback, and been given the required funds without a quibble.

As the personbus ground itself to a stationary position, an enormous hiss sounded as Frankie released the spare heat and steam. The novel approach the brothers had taken in harnessing the ancient might of coal to the modern efficiency of electricity wasn't without its faults; if the transient wet-cell ever reached full charge there was a reasonable chance it could explode. Hence Frankie's wise decision to dump the furnace whilst the battery wasn't being actively used.

Ms Larton had already opened the carriage door. She strode towards the main house, where a gentleman was waiting. Top hat and tails; he appeared to be an individual of high standing.

"Eyes up, Frankie, we've got company", Esau growled under his breath. His brother was an absolute natural with engines. Humans? Not so much. Better if he remained out of sight, at least until they found out more.

Esau unfolded himself from the cockpit, taking a moment to straighten his cap and brush his waistcoat. He glued a professional smile onto his face, and marched towards the couple at the foot of the steps.

The gentleman was looking over the personbus with a quizzical expression. He seemed unconvinced by Ms Larton's animated speech. She was currently whirling her arms around her like a poorly articulated ballerina.

"Ah, Mr Jones", she beckoned, "I was just explaining to Sir Humphrey that your machine would be just the ticket for grounds management. Don't you agree?"

Taken somewhat in surprise by the sudden question, "Err... well, I mean, yes!" Esau spluttered, "That is to say, yes, the vehicle has a number of attachments. Certainly we have considered tools for agricultural or grass cutting uses..."

The tall gentleman frowned at Esau's stumbling explanation, "Fine, I will give you the opportunity to... impress me".

Such was the manner that, three days later, they found themselves on the pristine fields of the Manchester Cricket Club, seated in the personbus with their new even-more-experimental-than-usual "Grassvator" attachment.

"Frankie! Heave to!", yelled Esau. The deep pulsing began, as the battery connected and the tracks began to inch them forward.

He grasped the newest, shiniest lever, and pulled it down to the "Engage" position. An ear-splitting whine began, and seven blades began to spin, moving lower, nearer and nearer to the perfect geometry of the club's pitch.

Esau looked behind them, where - to his good surprise - a lower trim to the lawn was revealed!

Then they lurched over a small rise.

Which jolted them *just* enough to cause the leading blade to collide energetically with the soil, and began to cut in with a screeching noise.

Esau frantically grabbed the lever, but it was too late - the momentum of the vehicle turned the spinning blades into a rotavating whirlwind, and burrowed them down, *through* the perfect turf.

By the time they had stopped, irrecoverable damage had been done. In the distance, an irate Sir Humphrey could be seen marching towards them, fists balled and yelling.

Esau sighed. It was time, once more, to ask Ms Larton for assistance.

You can't sail a hurricane. That's wha' everyone says. Can't do it.

We'd been runnin' back from Jamaica. Holds full of sugar, low in the water. In a big three-masted bark like *Emerald*, that's one heavy madam.

That time of year, a squall can become a storm any time. We'd passed *Vigilant* on her way in; she'd warned us things were getting fierce, but, y'all know how it is. If you turn tail every time the wind blows in the Gulf, you'll die a poor man.

So we sailed on, and the wind spins on up with us. Well, "You git what you git, and don't throw a fit", as they say, so we threw a prayer up, reefed her down and carried on.

Soon you couldna' hear a word. Just the air raging so hard around us that each and every line started whistlin'. The mate comes to me, "This is too much, we gotta heave to!" He had to shout - even then most all I could do was see his lips move.

Ah was about to turn us about, when the bosun runs in, all spun up too. "We're takin' on water Cap! Comin' in fast!".

We were stuck between a rock and Aunt Sue. Way it were, we had no time to turn back to port - we'd sink without a sight of shore. But carry on, we'd risk the masts, the rigging, the sails, the whole blessed ship. It was all or nothing.

"Gotta be on", Ah decided. And on we went. It got worse, much worse. Lost two hands overboard, and we'll not trust the masts until a carpenter's looked them over, but we made it. Splintered and broke, but we made it.

You can't sail a hurricane, they say - but we did.

Open drawers

No matter how hard you try, you can't escape from them. They get in through the tiniest of holes, like mice. Intelligent, malevolent mice. You have two options: moving house or murder.

You don't want to move. Not again.

And yet, it *is* murder. It has to be. They think, they talk, they scheme. It's not killing a human, but it's killing something self-aware.

When you'd left your last house behind, you'd spent the extras. Purpose built housing development, "No infestations here", the Sales Agent had promised. He'd had a nervous smile, but then, wouldn't you? Flogging houses in a world where goblins exist, invade and destroy dwellings?

The time before that, you'd naively attempted *friendship*. All those tired old conservatives, they weren't open-minded like you. You were sure that a hand of compassion would build a bridge, "There's room for both our kinds in this home", that sort of thing.

Then they ate your cat. One day, Pebbles was padding warily around the kitchen, next day no cat.

Just a collar and... a thank you note.

A thank you note. You, you just couldn't quite tell. Was it a sincere thank you, for the gift of feline food, or were they throwing it in your face, a brazen, sarcastic attack?

You couldn't take it, after that. You moved the next week, lasted 6 months... until the rustling began. The scuffles. The open doors, moved chairs, the ornately carved furniture. More and more footsteps in the night. The sudden loss of electrical power in your bedroom, and the smell of smoke. The question was not "could they start a fire". It was "would they"?

So this time, you went *Goblin Proof*™ . An electric membrane around the entire estate, anti-miscreant wall conductors. Just enough energy to *dissuade* the little invaders. Not hurt them, not seriously. The literature was very clear on that. So was the legislation. No one in Government wants that conversation. "Is it murder?". Best to avoid the act rather than deal with the mess of needing to define it.

And yet, you can't stop thinking about it. At first, you believe it is a passing whimsy. A fleeting thought. But it keeps coming back to you.

It doesn't matter, you tell yourself. It's not an issue you'll ever have to worry about. Until the house down the road burns down, right down, one night. Until the man with the nervous smile, smiles again. "Not actually guaranteed, no", he says. "More 'Goblin Resistant', to be completely accurate".

Then, the thoughts come back with a crash. What if the power was increased, just a little? It might stop them... completely.

You might never have gone beyond idle thought, if the noises hadn't begun. Little footsteps. A drawer, open in the morning. It had *definitely* been closed the evening before.

Sleep stops abruptly then. Totally. Wide awake. Listening. Waiting.

Some people begin to leave, but most stay. The ones who stay, something changes. They didn't seem to be affected, not physically, not by the infestations. Something else has gone though, in their eyes. You recognise it from the mirror. Something has broken.

You work it out, eventually. With so many wakeful nights, it is inevitable. Laying there, listening, waiting, until your conscience can't hold you any more.

Such a simple change, in the end. Almost as if the manufacturers want you to do it. Like flicking a switch. Non-lethal to lethal. Deterrence to death.

The noises stop. No more open drawers. No more home invaders.

And you can sleep again. You know that's wrong. You should be awake. But you sleep.

A thick crust of decay lay on every part of him. Slowly, tiny rivulets began to trickle down. The figure hadn't moved, but the scene had somehow *changed* - like an oil painting that you realise was a photo all along.

The skin on his face was more leather than flesh. It was ancient and lined, with pursed, waxen lips. They drew a single, hesitant breath. His chest shuddered, and more dust shook off in a shower of mortification.

One eye opened, abruptly, with a confused expression - the look of a man sleeping so long he'd forgotten how to move - before the other eyeball reluctantly joined it in a half-set scowl. His eyes were rheumy, even the whites a jaundiced brown.

How long?, he thought. How long, and why am I awakened?

A noise echoed from deep within the house.

The sound was familiar to him, if only his aching brain would focus. The sound of steps? Foot. Steps.

Of course. That foul malediction had roused him, because another mortal had entered his home. His lair.

And now he had a chance, once more, to steal the youth of another. To remake his own. The cracked lips curled into a smile.

CRITICAL
MALFUNCTION
IMMINENT

The isolation manifold reverberated.

That, in itself, was not a huge problem. Engines are filled with moving parts; spinning, whizzing, rumbling. Even in the most finely tuned machines, unexpected vibrations can happen.

Unfortunately, for the soon-to-be-extinct crew of the *Cymnion*, the reason for the reverberation was a blockage. Specifically, a blockage in one of the tiny valves that are vital for safe functioning of an Exclusion Drive.

Already lost in the jargon? Thought so. Jumping through quantum-space is a familiar process now, but the intricate details of the science are not. Just as people from the twentieth century would ride in cars without the faintest idea what a cylinder head was, quantum travel is only understood by a technically-minded minority.

In short, through the application of an impossible-to-visualise equation, an Exclusion Drive filters "real" space. It peels away the void in the immediate vicinity of a spacecraft and compresses that nothingness into tiny pellets of anti-matter. This "isolates" the ship in a bubble of quantum dimensionality - known as "q-space".

The pellets of anti-matter are spat out and harmlessly cleared through the isolation manifold, to be stored for later disposal. Simple. Well, sort of, once you get past the brain melting physics I've skipped over. But it works, it allows humanity to travel the stars, and it's relatively safe.

Unless the isolation valves get blocked.

Now, normally, a range of extremely sensitive sensors in the cockpit will warn of such a blockage. It takes around an hour for an antimatter build-up to reach the sort of critical mass that can, for instance, utterly vaporise a ship and everything within 20 kilometres of it. However, by the time things start reverberating, much of that safety margin has already elapsed.

The issue, in this circumstance, was two-fold. Firstly, no one in the cockpit was paying attention. Or, more accurately, no one in the cockpit was paying attention to safety alarms. The 57 minutes that the blockage beacon had been flashing had, unfortunately for the crew, coincided with the live broadcast of the Trans-Galactic ZeroG Basketball Finals.

Whilst top tier basketball, especially freed from its prior constraints of Earth, gravity and bans on player-cybernetic enhancements, was undoubtedly a fine spectacle, it probably wasn't worth dying for.

The second issue was that, during those fateful three minutes after the crew had become aware of the blockage alarm, they failed to collaboratively agree on anything.

Rizzle screamed, "What do we do?", the warning lights colouring her face scarlet.

Still with one eye on the TGZG game, Morgan grunted, "Dunno. Can't it wait?".

Azza was frantically flicking through the user manual. They were holding it upside down, a sign that terror was taking the lead over strategic planning.

Rizzle looked, wide eyed, at the display. All the normal displays were now replaced with a message in block capitals, "CRITICAL MALFUNCTION IMMINENT". She physically grabbed Morgan's head, wrenching his vision towards the cockpit. His expression changed to mouth-hanging-open shock, just in time to register the countdown reaching zero.

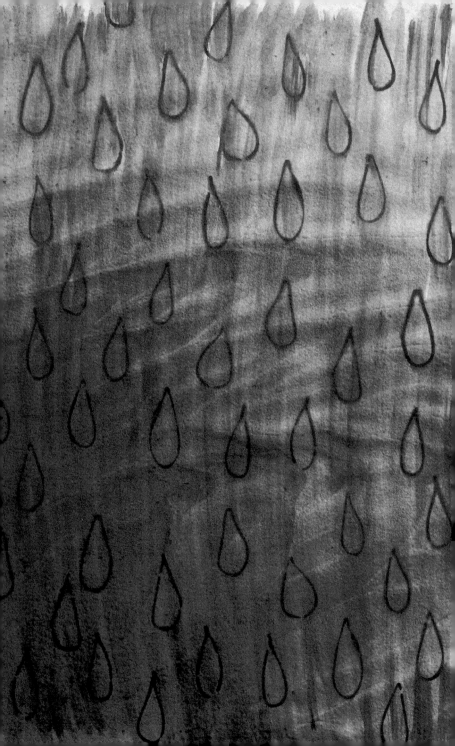

The clouds were dark and angry. Rain hammered against the thin tarpaulin, with just a crack of sky daggering through the thin slit at the front of the tent. A bad day for being outside, but a good one for hiding.

Suze packed her sleeping bag tightly. She was going to risk leaving the camo shelter in place, but everything else needed to come with her.

If her equipment was lost, she had no idea how she would manage to find more.

She crouched and shuffled out through the undergrowth for several metres, cautiously raising herself under the cover of a bushy shrub. She briefly scrutinised her camp site. No, not obvious, not unless you knew exactly where it was already. She scanned the surrounding terrain. Empty. She marched on.

The village was only a few miles, and it seemed the bad weather had scared away nearly everyone else. She reached the burnt church on market street, and ducked into the shadows by the remaining steps. Not a moment too soon, either, as a patrol appeared out of thin air and stormed suspiciously past her hiding place.

Somehow, as she waited for the militia to pass, the rain got even heavier. It became difficult to see, with the intensity of water falling on her face. Pouring tears, just without the salt.

She ran now, keen to minimise time potentially exposed. She bounced from alcove to alcove, pausing under trees and inside bushes.

Still slightly breathless, she got to the market. A few stalls of food, disgruntled stallholders and more militia than customers. The remains of a building smoked nearby. Perhaps there had been another outbreak, or just some kind of unrest; either way, the town was on high alert. Subterfuge wasn't going to work here. She would need to grab and run.

Suze waited, as several of the militia slunk into a shelter to drink some steaming beverages they had just purchased – or, more likely, intimidated – from a scowling stallkeeper. She walked then, hood over her face, enough to keep the rain off and slightly conceal her face, but not enough to appear to be intentionally hiding. Just another scared human.

She began at one edge, apparently looking over the range of tools at the first stall.

"How much for the hacksaw?", she asked.

Whilst the bald man behind the table quoted an unreasonable price, she silently palmed a small wooden box onto the table. Pre-wound earlier, the timer began. She had around a minute before it went off.

She moved, quickly but calmly, to the food stall on the other side of the square. She had been there just long enough to appear to be legitimately deciding on a purchase when a high pitched clanging began at the tool stand. Stall holders spun round, distracted. The militia began to walk over, to where the bald man was shouting and gesticulating.

Still calmly, but now with the knowledge that she had only seconds to act, Suze scooped an armful of food, dropping it into her open bag. She managed a second load before the straw hatted woman behind the stall noticed and shouted, "What on earth are you doing?! STOP! THIEF!!"

Suze sprinted, feet rupturing deep puddles as she skimmed out through the town.

Then, just as she reached the ruined church, at the worst possible moment, another patrol appeared.

She wheeled to the left, down an empty road. A dead end. She reached the wall. Beyond was the river, swollen to a rage by the rains. Deep, fast. Dangerous. Angry voices came nearer. Dangerous.

She closed her eyes and jumped.

"Errrk!"

A few more seconds of smooth rolling, and then, again, it cries out. "Errrk!"

It's a drawn out wail, like the bearings themselves are calling out in pain.

I try to ignore it. "Errrk!" But it comes so often, every so many rotations. It is inevitable. "Errrk!"

Worse, it's a punishment for moving. Vegging out and watching TV all day, you'd never hear it at all. But you decide to go out for some fresh air, and... "Errrk!"

Like so many innovations brought in under the guise of *Progress* the wheels have some immediate benefits, but ever so many more disadvantages. The squeaking as the bearings start to seize up is hardly the worst of it. The pain, for example, never really truly fades. Nor has anyone in the Council apparently considered just how many homes include stairs. Feet are a much better fit for that particular job.

Still, they have increased productivity; according to the statistics produced by the Council, anyway. Yes, that's right, the same people who mandated surgery for every one of us, they're the ones who get to check whether they made the right decision. Thankfully - according to them at least - it was.

My fax machine whirrs. A fax machine in every dwelling *has* made it easier for the Council to contact us with their mandates, can't argue with that one.

"Errrk!" I try to ignoring the phantom pain in my right big toe. I know there's nothing there, but it feels so real. Reading the print out is a good distraction.

It turns out to be an effective distraction, not a good one.

"Progress 142/20: for added strength and productivity, all workers will have one hand replaced with techmechanical claw".

In despondent fury, I clench my fists. While I still can.

"It doesn't matter"

800 mystery green leaves

"Well, I don't think it matters, that's all".

"You don't think it matters?"

"No. I don't. I really don't".

"I'm not sure we should carry on then, if you aren't willing to..."

"Willing to what?!"

"You know what I'm saying".

"Yes, I do, but you clearly still want to say it".

"Fine. If you aren't willing to consider the full moral implications of this project, I'm not sure if I want to work with you on it any more."

"..."

"There's no point in scowling at me now, is there? If you can't even be bothered to have a conversation about the subject, why should I stick around?"

"Fine! Let's talk about it then".

"..."

"Well go on then! I thought this was some kind of vitally important topic for you to unpack. Unpack it!"

"Sometimes I forget what a thoroughly irritating human you are Greg"

"Irritating human *genius*, I'll have you know".

"Yes, yes. Of course I know. *Everyone* knows. You show new starters your Mensa certificate on their first day, just in case they don't work out that you're an utter prig on their own. I'm not bothered if your IQ is 180, you still have the emotional awareness of a loaf of bread."

"If a loaf of bread can get paid as much as me, I'm happy with the comparison. And it's 183 actually".

"Fine. *Well done!*"

"Thank you".

"That wasn't a... never mind. Okay, the project. I can't believe you really haven't considered the implications".

"Oh I have. I just don't think they matter".

"But, why not?"

"It will start with people's choice. No one will make them buy this stuff."

"Not at first, no, but it's going to snowball. You've seen the efficiency graphs - the plants grow hundreds of times faster than anything else. It won't take long for them to out-compete the entire worldwide agricultural economy."

"I know! Impressive, right?"

"Well, admittedly yes, but that means that choice will go out of the window when there's no other options available".

"Not immediately though. We need, what, seven years? To scale up, to meet that kind of truly global demand. Call it ten. We can only do that if there's money coming in?"

"Sure."

"And its not all coming from investors, is it?"

"No, I think the aim is already 50/50 sales by year two".

"Right. So the great unwashed will be choosing our food, our plants, our processes. They will be voting in their approval with the contents of their wallets. By the time we control the market, there will have been a decade of people preferentially selecting us over our competitors".

"They've made a choice then, that's your argument?"

"Sure. Choice, consent, call it what you want; they've had the option not to, and they've declined to use it."

"Okay. Say I accept that - and I'm not saying I do - that still leaves the addiction. Consuming the things we grow is physically addictive. We'll be creating a billion addicts."

"Irrelevant. Everyone is already addicted."

"They... what? Of course they aren't. How can they be addicted? We've not even launched yet."

"No, its true. Look - what is addiction?"

"...what? I mean, addiction? It's addiction! People addicted to things."

"Calm down. Just define it for me. Define the word 'addiction'".

"Okay, okay. Off the top of my head... so, addiction is when a human, or any animal I suppose, has a... a biological need for a substance... one that without they will have... some kind of physical symptoms of withdrawal?"

"Close enough. Physical and mental dependence on a substance is the usual line. So, are you addicted to anything currently?"

"No. Don't smoke, don't drink, don't use drugs".

"...don't eat?"

"Eat? Of course I eat. Everyone has to eat. I don't eat our product though..."

"Ignore that. Everyone has to eat. So everyone is physically and mentally dependent on food?"

"I mean, yes? I suppose so".

"And you mentioned the idea of withdrawal?"

"Well yes. The withdrawal from the compounds in the plants can be fatal! And it is intrinsically linked to the fast growth! Can't have one without the other..."

"No, ignore our plants. Just generally, what happens if you don't eat food."

"I get... hungry?"

"Right, and then, if you still don't eat?"

"I run out of energy... I get weaker. I..."

"...die?"

"Well yes, if I completely stopped eating I *would* die..."

"So you have a physical dependence on a substance, and if you stop consuming it you'll die?"

"Well, if you put it that way..."

"Then you are addicted to food. As is everyone. So when our food is the only food available, it will be irrelevant that it is also fatally addictive."

"Er... wow. I actually don't have a response to that".

"Exactly. It doesn't matter. Now get back to work."

5:20

Westclox

The sounds of a busy restaurant are pervasive. They seem to linger, beyond the actual experience. They live on in your psyche.

That's how Velvet found it anyway. So used to being told off for chopping the shallots "slower than an actual retard", or of being regularly physically assaulted under the guise of "well that's what happens when you get in the way", it was hard to relax at home. Or anywhere. Call it PTSD, call it stress, call it *his life being ruined by that monster*; ultimately the quasi-auditory feeling of being shouted at at all times was hard to get away from.

The alarm blared out again. Velvet slammed a hand against it. Off, but too late. Everyone hates the noise of their alarm clock, but the similarity to the order buzzer was too much. His heart was racing now, sweat starting to bead in his temples.

He swung his legs out of bed, and reluctantly dressed. Once finished, he glanced at the time again. 5:20am. Too early, especially for a job that underpaid so unashamedly. Turgid cornflakes were consumed. Fuel for the gruelling shift ahead. Then out the door.

Every step that took him nearer to *La Dauphiné* was progressively heavier. Harder. Even so - and however much he wished otherwise - he arrived. Ten minutes to six. After all, "if you can't be bothered to be early, we can't be bothered to employ you". Why did that work? Some days he *yearned* to be fired. To be free. And yet... here he was. Ten minutes early, for the prize of non-existent praise.

He clocked in his time card. A physical memento of his obsequious obedience. A sullen nod from Karn, also arriving. She worked Entrées, he was a (very junior) Commis Chef, but there was no difference to their treatment. Chef de Cuisine Leon was rarely concerned with anything beyond the two Os: Orders and the Owner. As long as dishes went out on time - and *La Dauphiné*'s financial beneficiaries were not on site - junior staff were simply a test track for his speeding wheels of ego and cruelty.

Velvet donned his whites and arrived on station. It was meticulously clean, as usual - night time clean down was "more important than saying goodbye to your nan", so that was never skipped. Velvet winced inwardly, as the thought triggered memories of the two very real family funerals he had missed due to uncancellable shifts.

He noted Karn was already prepping vegetables, getting that little bit ahead. The dream was to have a full station of ingredients ready before Leon blew past your area, for the unreal hope of a brief nod - or even, ludicrously, a "good job". It wasn't just about having the perfect ingredients, quantities and proportions. There was an art, a sublime perfection that went beyond words. Karn usually beat him in that too, showed him up, winning both the race to superiority in skill and in something ineffable too.

Not today. Velvet waited, until Karn's unavoidable trip to the cooler. Gazpacho starter today; she'd have to go.

In that brief window, he walked, slow but purposeful. A man with a valid reason. No one would question.

He drizzled the small bottle all over Karn's delicate piles, and returned to his own focused work. There was a moment of apprehension, as he considered the outcome of peanut oil on Leon's allergy. It wouldn't kill him, no - the adrenaline pen in Velvet's other pocket ensured that. But praise would be due. Rare, sweet praise.

He knew it wasn't worth it, not really. But he wanted it anyway.

```
program: leaving nothing.
buffer 600... loaded.
nanopunk... loaded.
betrayal... loaded.

next command? _
```

Leaving nothing
600 nanopunk betrayal

Eliezer tightened his eyepieces fiercely. Everything he did these days was fierce. He closed doors fiercely, he ate dinner fiercely, he even disconnected from head-calls fiercely - which usually left him with a migraine.

The headgear he wore was enabling him to operate the Minimiser on his workstation; you see, Eliezer worked as a "micro-adjuster". Specifically, he was part of a team of specialists that fine-tuned communication receptors in nanobots. Important stuff, given that every human has millions of bots inside them. However, since the breakup, he'd been slacking; in fact, he'd lost interest in the entire project. Life in general had dimmed in appeal.

His mood had been further cratered by the findings of his recent "investigations". As a privileged user, he had access to the contents of transmissions between the micro-machines. It was necessary, in order to troubleshoot and improve their communicators. It was, sadly, also possible to use such privileges to eavesdrop on one's ex-girlfriend, and discover that: she had a new boyfriend; and also that the new boyfriend had been seeing her for 2 months *even though she only broke up with Eliezer 2 weeks ago.* Eliezer slammed a hand onto the desk at the memory. He did so particularly fiercely.

Some people respond to relationship breakdown with depression. Isolation. Misery. Such events often cause mental health disturbances, and in the worst cases this can even lead to suicidal thoughts. Eliezer was suffering from all those symptoms, and his coping strategy involved viewing it all through a red mist of rage.

In truth? He had decided he was ready to die. Disappointingly, he had decided to do so in as destructive a way as possible, inflicting as much collateral damage as was within his power.

Now, to understand just how prodigious Eliezer's annihilatory potential was, you need to know how nanotech operates; especially compared to the circuit-based technology you might be familiar with.

Instead of one set of planned purposes for a piece of equipment, bots are able to adjust to an infinite range of different tasks. They can clump together or co-ordinate for different effects, exponentially increasing their capacity. Hence the ability for the same nanobots to exist within human auditory canals and connect conversations between individuals thousands of miles apart; to be instrumental in making sure that driver-less vehicles do not collide with one another; ensuring that vegetables in your fridge do not undergo lipid oxidation and stay fresh indefinitely; and endless other applications. They are part of *everything*.

Now, years of nanobot assembly coding had left Eliezer with quiet mastery of its intricacies.

His adjustments were simple in concept, horrendous in application: he wrote a firmware update. These packets of code are passed between bots, slowly spreading through the world in a cloud of wireless instruction.

The initialisation instructions for each bot were replaced with two commands:

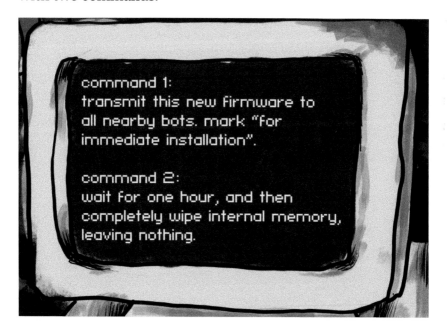

```
command 1:
transmit this new firmware to
all nearby bots. mark "for
immediate installation".

command 2:
wait for one hour, and then
completely wipe internal memory,
leaving nothing.
```

He connected through the Minimiser, watching as instructions were rewritten onto a captured bot. He paused. Once the Minimiser released the nanobot, the tiny machine would activate, and the process would be unstoppable.

His contemplation was interrupted by a memory of his girlfriend's infidelity. He could see her face. He could visualise the two of them together.

His finger stabbed at the "release" button. Rather fiercely, as you would expect.

Sixty-one minutes later the nano-clump pacemaker in his left ventricle disintegrated, and Eliezer's heart stopped beating. It was three more minutes before jetcars began to fall from the sky, but he was no longer alive to see that.

An icy mist rose from the recombination chamber. The door hissed, and swung open.

Verran-cussler braced against a rusted girder. They weren't quite sure if they were holding on for support or getting ready to hide.

The vapour faded away. Nothing moved.

Their next action required careful deliberation. If the creature had survived, it might not appreciate any sudden movement.

A deep, shuddering breath echoed out from the chamber.

Verran-cussler hesitated and then stepped out. Face to face with their creation. It was *perfect*.

"Master..." it said, each syllable an iceberg calving.

"Come", beckoned Verran-cussler, "We have work to do..."

Leverö Öperk Moritus

500 historical betrayal

A thornraven took flight, letting out a deep cry as it did so. It swooped low over the battlements, its dark shadow barely registering against the wet rock.

The castle stood against the tragic sky, silhouetted by the half-light of the ne'er setting sun. Whether by curse or trick of nature, the Working Empire had been in perpetual twilight for more time than any could remember.

Watchers on the high walls looked out for invaders, for Dracorae or any threat to the iron rule of peace on the land. Each Watcher wore a uniform of rusted, worn chain-mail, and a helmet with the distinctive slashed visors of the Empire.

Norculse could see them, from where he stood, uncomfortably. The wind was biting today, so wretched that his fingers ached. There was no shelter for him.

Below, in the courtyard, he could hear Seeders setting to work, doing their best to persuade the reluctant soil to produce food. Each year this proved harder, with barely enough grown for the meagre ration provided.

He closed his eyes, hoping this would grant him a moment of relief from the burning cold. Somewhere else would be others, the Childers and the Cookers, every person of Age assigned to their lifelong role.

It was a defining characteristic of the Empire, the Four Roles, based on an ancient promise - *Leverö Öperk Moritus*. Live. Work. Die. Every member of the Empire with their energy expended and needs fulfilled.

A sudden sharp pain tore through his leg. Norculse looked down. A thornraven was there, its toothed beak savagely tearing into the meat of his calf. He couldn't move out of the way, so instead he screamed in anguish and frustration. The vile bird tilted its head, looking at him with amused indifference, before bending its neck to wrench at his flesh again.

He bellowed in his impotence as the pain took him again. With no other option, he began to spit at the bird, his parched mouth hesitatingly lending him moisture. Finally, the cursed crow took flight, either put off by his spittle, or simply having eaten its fill.

A jeer from below turned his attention away from his ruined limb. A crowd was gathering.

"Where's your work, you filthy Topper?", shouted a one-armed man, face marred by a poorly healed burn.

"No work, no life!" a faceless voice called out, a cry quickly picked up by the rest of the mob.

Norculse flinched, as a stone hit his forehead. Soon a shower of projectiles hammered against his naked body. Tied firmly by both hands and feet, he was powerless to dodge, each impact a further sting to his mutilated dignity.

Leader. An empire needed Leaders, if it were to function, to evolve, to *survive*, but the angry mob repudiated this. They saw his dedication as a betrayal, a refusal to fulfil his part of the agreement that bound them all.

The tone of the crowd had darkened, chanting now the ancient promise:

Leverö Öperk Moritus.

Live.

Work.

Die.

The changes were so slight that, at first, no one even noticed. Let's be honest here: politicians aren't the most beloved of creatures. And being in power does *wear* at a person. Tony Blair was the youngest Prime Minister in a century, but after ten years at the helm he was definitely crinkling at the edges. So when Harold Kreak was elected, his leathery skin was par for the course, along with his close-set eyes and indistinguishable moral compass.

The Cabinet was rapidly filled, as is the norm, with like-minded chums of the PM. Looking back - with the benefit of hindsight - there was a clear visual similarity, a yellow eyed reptilian homogeneity. At the time though, it was unremarkable and thus unremarked.

It was the publication of their white paper *"On the Rights of Animals"* that lit a fire. Masquerading as a food safety welfare bill, it had - artfully hidden within sub-clauses - a paragraph describing the "unassailable sentience and self-evident citizenry of the Saurian and Ophidian inhabitants of the United Kingdom". Missed by all, and soon progressed to a Bill, it proposed human-level rights for snakes and lizards.

Rights of Animals passed into law on the 19th of September. The next day a Downing Street press conference was held with a clatter of cameras in the Rose Garden.

"Good morning Sssscitizens!", proclaimed a sibilant Kreak. His streaks of greying hair had gone, replaced with patterned green and red scales right over his head, and down the creases of his neck. Surrounding him were his cabinet, an assortment of crocodilian creatures, unblinkingly staring down the cameras. A united front of political, zoological upheaval.

"Today, a new order of ssossciety beginss!", he hissed, to nods of approval from the surrounding figures. I watched it live. I couldn't stop watching. The Home Secretary, now with a striking near-blue tinge to his skin, was artfully licking his own eyes with a huge green tongue. The entire spectacle was simply alien.

From that day they enacted their master plan. It began with equal rights for lizardfolk - the group noun they requested we call them, although some sectors of society termed their own, less genteel terminology - but soon degenerated, imperceptibly, into a two-tier system. A system with mammals *firmly* at the bottom.

The expected fight back from the populace? It never took place. Firstly, the dissemination of the lizards throughout power structures in society had clearly been long-planned and systematic. From politicians to police, judges to jails - overnight almost every authority was revealed to be reptile-run. The media lurched at the same time, re-calibrating into a limited spectrum between wildly pro-lizard at one end and bias hidden cleverly behind left-wing facade at the other end (The Guardian's series on "The positive environment impact of being cold-blooded" was particularly persuasive).

Secondly, no one was quite sure what the lizards *ate*. People began to go missing, and lizards began to get fatter. There were no clear links between those two points, no public statements, no video footage, no actual proof that lizards were feasting on the flesh of humanity; just the ever-growing suspicion, one that became more sinister the longer it remained unconfirmed.

Eventually, almost unbelievably, things stabilised. The population, fed by constant propaganda from government, media, police, social networks, grew to accept their position, our position, as humanity, playing second fiddle to dinosaurs in suits.

For those of us who yearned to fight, to organise, to protest? Well, they never seem to last long. The *surveillance ssstate*, it's called, in hush tones, by those brave enough to discuss such things. There's never been any public confirmation, but, ultimately, our scaly overlords have total control, total power and... very sharp teeth. People continue to disappear, and the lizards continue to get fatter. Nowadays some of them can hardly even move, wedged in place like Jabba the Hutt, sending hatchlings out to manage their business.

Don't be fooled. They might look chubby but they are always, *always* in control.

Maybe one day we will be free, but I'm not comfortable talking about it any more. The walls have ears. Or ear slits, anyhow. Anyone asks, I think they're great. Fantastic. Whatever keeps me off a plate.

Just as planned

A buzzing noise was the only sound of the alarm. We were made. Still, we'd been ready for that. I started to run for the guardrail, and vaulted over it with practised ease. It really was practised – I'd spent an hour jumping gates in the park a few weeks before.

I fell, just long enough to notice myself falling, and crashed into the water with a huge splash. I felt the buoyancy of my wet suit already pulling me up before I reached the bottom of my trajectory: I burst from the surface, ready to go. The jet-skis were only a few lengths away. I scrambled onto mine, looking around for Nick. Behind us, lights were turning on, with raised voices shouting orders at each other. The crew of *The Eventual Hope* were waking up to the fact that their security had been breached.

A breathless Nick climbed onto the ski next to me,

and we fired up both motors in unison. There was no time for conversation; the first gunshots sounded from behind us as we weaved our way away from the ship. A bullet hole appeared, uncomfortably close to my right foot.

We tore on, and the shots continued. Another gunman joined the first, thankfully both armed with pistols, as far as I could tell from the sound. We were soon at the edge of their range, although not quite soon enough, as a cluster of holes appeared on my fuselage, and my motor seized with an abrupt, complaining crunch. It was probably dead, and there was no time for troubleshooting. Nick noticed my lack of motion, and swung back round to me; I leapt onto the back of his jet-ski and we were off again.

Now the bullets were no longer coming, a silence was left, quickly replaced with the ominous buzz of multiple humming motors. We knew that the Hope had their own range of small craft, but we'd banked on our choice of hugely overpowered jet-skis to give us the edge. That edge had probably gone now that I was having to piggyback.

Freed from staring at the ocean ahead, I spun round to see what we were going to have to deal with. Two Zodiacs appeared, each with six black clad goons perched jauntily inside, and two jet-ski outriders. Fourteen people, in other words, chasing the two of us. And they had *lots* of guns.

A bullet whistled past, disappearing into a nearby wave. I tapped Nick on the shoulder insistently, "Dude, I'm going to need some firepower!"

He turned his head, whilst still focusing on the approaching shore ahead, and yelled "Seat-box".

I crouched, awkwardly – never an easy task in a tight wetsuit, on a full speed jet-ski, whilst trying to dodge a small arsenal, but I'm a modern woman; I've even survived the toilets at Reading Festival – and felt inside the seat box. A huge, bulky weapon was crammed in there. It had some kind of drum attached to it. I yelled back at Nick, "Nick?!"

"Yeah?!"

"Why the hell do we have a flipping Tommy Gun?!"

"It was cheap!"

I was lost for words, for a moment, at the sheer ridiculousness of the situation, but what choice was there but to make the best of it? I aimed the 1920s mobster weapon behind us. With a satisfying chadda chadda, it sprayed enough bullets to significantly hinder one of the jet-skis. It wasn't clear if I hit the rider, but the way he fishtailed into the business end of one of the Zodiacs - leaving them both dead in the water - was very satisfying.

That left just two watercraft chasing us. I swung to the second Zodiac, which was still closing on us, and fired again. The empty click I felt was very unsatisfying. I was out of bullets.

"Where do I get more ammo?"

"There's a spare drum in the other box!", shouted Nick, not even having the decency to sound apologetic for providing me with a weapon older than my Grandma.

Fumbling around, I eventually found the extra magazine, managing to eject and reload, cursing Nick and the circumstances of his birth under my breath as I did so. Shots from our pursuers continued to pepper around us, but I ignored them; there was nothing I could do about it.

Finally, I carefully took aim, feathering the trigger to allow myself a little more time to refocus my shots. The pilot of the Zodiac fell back with a, well, *dead* look on his face, and the boat curved off to the side. Only the jet-ski remained, and he appeared to be out of bullets. I had just demonstrated that reloading on a bucking jet-ski at 50mph is unpleasant; he seemed to be focusing on getting as close as possible instead

I fired at him several times, but each time the sea shifted beneath us, or him, and I missed. Then I was empty again.

By now Mr Jet-ski was metres away, and scowling. He began to sway level with us, planning on ramming us. The thing with a Tommy Gun, ridiculous as it is, it certainly has a decent weight behind it. I took aim, and carefully tossed it towards him. It clonked him on the head, and our final pursuer fell in the sea, arms waving.

"Shore is coming, Diane!", shouted Nick. We braced. Perhaps we would make it after all.

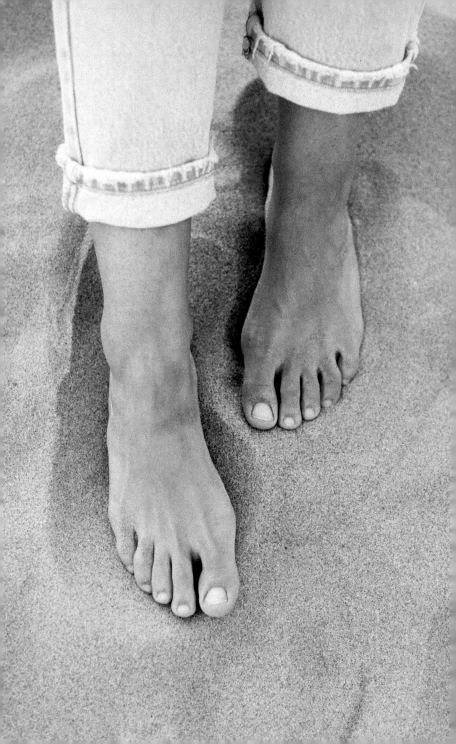

Uqalekisiwe

700 drama urban

She ran.

A howling wind surrounded her. The fine sand, ever-present, picked at her. Her footsteps were silent, a barefoot pad inaudible over the gale. Her eyes were stinging, mostly from the abrasive wind. Partly from her tears.

Lindelwa turned the dusty corner of Motlomelo Street, and tore off across the bush. It was quicker cutting past the vleiland - a natural deposit of salt pans on the edge of town - than taking the longer route out by the main road. More likely to avoid teasing that way too.

She itched her arm, the skin was flaking in her elbow crease. She shouldn't have got so burnt yesterday, but she'd been hiding on the beach from one of the gangs again. *Inkawa*, they'd taunted her. White monkey.

Birds circled far ahead, looking down. The bright blue near-turquoise of the vleiland was vibrant and huge. The tiny figure of Lindelwa picked slowly past them, from above visible as little more than a hat with pink feet poking out beneath.

It was clear no one was following her, so she slowed down, still breathing heavily. Just being free of the suffocating confines of Sizamile was enough.

Sizamile. "We tried" it means, in Xhosa. What kind of name for a home was that? "Not very hard", it felt like. She wasn't sure of the details, but she knew there was a half-forgotten, turbulent history for the area she and her family lived. Once a more affluent district, it was now the poorest part of town, where the least desirable were located.

The least desirable. A good place for her. In a country so conflicted by race, it was ironic to be basically white, and yet less desirable than the darkest skinned of her family. Albinism was the scientific name for it, but the Amadoda who drank outside the shabeen all day had another word; "Uqalekisiwe". Cursed.

The salt pans were past now, and she was walking through the dilapidated industrial region. Old Utatomkhulu Jonga used to talk about this area being a thriving hub of activity, back when the diamond mines were paying out and the harbour was still busy. Nowadays it was as threadbare as the rest of Port Nolloth.

The tarmac on Main Road was warm. Busier too. She usually avoided busy areas. Lindelwa could feel the usual interested glances. A small child staring. People noticing the unusual. She pulled her hat down lower, trying to reduce her peripheral vision.

And then, it happened. Inevitable. She should have crossed over earlier, but it was too late. A group of her schoolmates. A gang. Hanging around outside the Usave, eating bags of Nik-Naks and looking for something to do. Someone to pick on. She averted her eyes, but it was too late.

"Hey, whitey!", one of them crowed. It was Ana Nowell, one of the coloured girls in her class, and a total cow.

Everyone else joined in, "How is your tan going?", one Xhosa boy yelled, with several others making mocking gestures. They were a mixed bunch; white, black, coloured, all laughing at her. The rainbow nation might have hierarchies of race, but the black-girl-who-wasn't-black was clearly at the bottom.

Tears came again. She rushed past the group. A hand reached out and slapped at her. It was a playful movement, if mean-spirited, with little force behind it, but it hit her sore arm enough to sting. She flinched, and tripped on the kerb, landing face-down in the road. Behind, the giggling became an uproar.

She lay there, the cackling pricking at her self-worth like the sun did at her skin.

"Shut up, you idiots!", a voice cried out, "Shame on you!". The crowd murmured back, defensively.

"Are you okay Lindie?", the voice, quieter now. Lindelwa lifted her head.

It was Vicky. Lovely, friendly Vicky. The tanned Afrikaans girl smiled at her, and reached out a hand. "Ignore them", she said, and stuck out her tongue at the gang.

Lindelwa rose carefully to her feet. "Let's go to the Spar and get a trifle!", said Vicky.

The jeering voices faded away, dissolved by friendship.

They walked on the beach. They ate trifle.

They laughed and listened to the waves. The sand warmed her toes.

Community development

The street felt sweaty, under the weight of those hot, humid night-times you sometimes get in July. The sodium orange of London's ever-present light pollution had flooded everything to a dingy sepia.

A taped notice fluttered halfheartedly on a lamp post. It was difficult to read, the result of repeatedly being subjected to rain, but the title was still clear enough -"Planned demolition, prior to construction of multiple occupancy dwellings".

Opposite the smeared paper sat a darkened building. A squat postwar relic, its tatty walls were made from large segments of prefabricated concrete. Altogether, the boarded up windows, faded paintwork and rusting metal roofing gave the impression that it was cowering; trying to hide from the death penalty that had been cruelly sellotaped near enough for all to see.

Petitions had failed to convince the planning committee's construction-coveting hearts. The need for new housing outweighed any thought of the trickle of misfits still using the community centre. It was time for progress to have its turn.

A high-pitched beeping cut through the heavy air. The yellow-tinged street flashed amber as a vehicle reversed, warning strobes spinning at each high corner of the large truck. The steady rumble echoed off the surrounding buildings as the JCB shuddered to a halt in front of the dormant community centre.

A door slammed.

"Think we'll do it?", a gruff voice. Older. Male.

"We've got to." Female. Young. "There's no other options left".

Sparks bounced in the gutter, as the man threw aside his dog-end, still lit. The bright glow began to fade.

"When do the others get here?", the man said. From behind, all that was visible of him was a dark cap and a high vis jacket.

The woman turned, searched further up the road. The vehicle lights alternated her between shadow and heavily-contrasted ochre. She was young, probably mid-thirties. "They are nearby, they'll come when I call them. No point in having them here until we know if this is a fool's errand or not".

"Fine". The door slammed again. The woman stood back as the huge vehicle engaged its selector grabs; a massive pair of opposing claws. The engine roared as the linkage rose, positioning the jaws either side of the building's heavy steel roofing, like a Tyrannosaurus ready to bite.

The driver looked over to the woman, waiting. She nodded.

It was now or never.

The grabs tore the sheeting off the roof with a rending shriek. Spinning to the side, the cabin suspended high over the road, the JCB's claws released the roofing with a crash. It sounded like someone falling over in a drum showroom.

"Well, that's the neighbours woken," muttered the woman. Even as she said it, a light flicked on above a nearby shop. Another one followed. Another. She grimaced, then shrugged it off. They'd anticipated this.

She raised a walkie-talkie to her mouth, "Big bird here. Time to collect the chicks, over".

A hiss rattled out of the speaker. An indistinct "Roger!" squawked out.

The JCB had continued taking the metal layers off, and was now beginning to pull apart the thick, interlocked walls of the main structure. Normally clamped together with huge rusted bolts, the connections had been covertly removed over the previous two nights. All that held them in place was gravity - a not inconsiderable force, since each block weighed nearly a ton.

A distant rumbling solidified into five heavy trucks roaring down the road. One parked by the large digger, first in line to receive the pieces being removed from the building.

The noise of massive chunks of concrete being loaded onto the resonating bed of an empty truck was extraordinary. The woman stepped back, and looked down the street to see nearly every light on. Several doors were open, with people, angry, in pyjamas, stepping out to accost them. She put on her high hat, gave a nod to the driver of the nearest truck, and walked over to the nearest resident.

"How can I help, Ma'am?", she asked, as if the sound of nocturnal Armageddon behind them would be of no note to anyone.

"What are you doing? It's two in the morning!". This lady had her hair in curlers and was near apoplectic in rage.

"I'm sorry Ma'am, but the community centre has been scheduled for demolition, and there have been protesters threatening to intervene. The council has given us permission to proceed at an... unorthodox... time to avoid public disruption".

"To *avoid* disruption?!!! What in Bell's name do you call all this?!!". The lady raised her arms, already having to shout just to be heard over the unearthly din.

At this point, the police arrived, announcing their presence with a single bleat of their siren. The woman in the hard hat repeated her calm explanation, gently inviting the police to contact her supervisor and/or the council.

Of course, the council offices were firmly shut at this point in the night, but, contacted by phone, the supervisor confirmed the story in a firm and authoritative manner, "Absolutely approved, and needed in order to stop the protesters causing any more fuss".

Eventually, the police backed down, forming a cordon and ushering residents back to bed "All approved yes. In the best interests of all, please return to your homes".

Loading the trucks took just under two hours, in the end. The woman thanked the lead police officer, bidding them a cheerful "good night", then got into the cab with the last driver.

"Should be there in five minutes". The driver spoke with eerily familiar tones. In fact, he sounded identical to the voice of the "supervisor" who had reassured the police previously.

Unloading the centre onto the scrap land they'd managed to buy should be plain sailing. By the time anyone official realised, the centre would be rebuilt, in a new location.

If you do it right, you can steal an entire building *and the police will help you do it.*

The woman relaxed, as the sepia streets passed by.

The Perfect Crime

200 crime mastery

The real trick, I feel, isn't avoiding being caught. That just leaves a smoking gun. Nor is it pretending no crime has been committed; inevitably someone will discover the misdeed and a perpetrator becomes wanted again.

No, the ideal method is to frame somebody else, and to do it so seamlessly and perniciously that no thought of innocence can be entertained. Any protest, any argument of "It wasn't me", sounds then more and more desperate: deluded almost.

Once this aim is achieved, every step in the legal process designed to stop a wrongdoer works instead in their favour.

The police will detain the fall-person and determinedly *stop looking* for the miscreant.

Courts will proclaim the guilt of the sentenced, thus declaring "Justice Served" and the whole matter firmly resolved. In doing so, the idea of revisiting the decision, of trying an alternate person; it all now fights against the inertia of that perfectly served justice.

There is, of course, a loser in this process. One innocent party; unfairly blamed, wrongly seized and unrighteously imprisoned. They really do get the rough end of the stick. And that, Your Honour, brings me to my opening argument - you see... *it really wasn't me!*

Solid gold

"My name is Will, and I'm a compulsive gambler".

That's what I say, every Wednesday evening in the dreary hall behind the Methodists in Bramcote. I'm a gambler. And yes, it is a problem.

I started, like so many people do, with scratch cards. They seem so simple, so easy, so *exciting*. Just take off that silver layer and you can win anything! I used to buy one most days, when I was picking up a newspaper or chewing gum, whatever. I'd done it for years, often made a tenner here or there, most often just won back my entry price. Or nothing. Usually nothing, looking back.

One day - I remember it clearly - I was outside the pub, using a coin to scratch off the coating. It was raining, just a bit, and I huddled up against a phone booth to keep the worst off. A moneybag symbol appeared, and then another one, then a third. I could barely hold still with the excitement, and then, yes, the last two were moneybags too!

You've never felt the rush, the tingling pleasure unless you've won big at least once. Hands trembling, I picked up the phone and called the number on the back.

I'd won. Three. Million. Pounds. Three million! Three, plus zero zero zero zero zero and zero. I couldn't breathe!

That should have been it, really. Set for life, buy a house, mortgage free forever, never need to work again. Looking back, I wish it had been.

It wasn't even that I was unwise with my investments. Some people buy a silly car, or a house they can't afford, ends up costing them more than they made. I was worse; I took a celebratory trip to Vegas.

I booked ahead, the "Supreme" package, at The Venture, one of the biggest hotels on the strip. Told them I'd just become a millionaire and wanted to celebrate. They met me at the airport with a limo and free champagne on ice! Took me back to my hotel room - it had a gold bathtub! More free champagne too! I started off my trip with a soak in the bubbles, and more than one glass of bubbly.

Then I headed downstairs to the casino itself. Have you ever been to one? I hadn't. They can be scary places, so many games you've only seen in movies, but have no idea how to play. The Venture had thought of everything - they provided me a staff member, Janine, to walk me round and explain everything. I offered her some champagne, but she just smiled and declined.

The evening was a blur, to be frank. The free drinks kept coming, and the money kept going. I played Craps, Poker,

Roulette, Blackjack, Pai Gow, Keno, everything they had. I remember winning, with cheers around me, and I remember losing, weeping into my glass.

And then I remember nothing. Until...

Bang! Bang! Bang!

A loud noise, too loud! I woke up, confused.

My head was pounding so badly, at first I thought it was just the blood pumping in my temples.

Boom! Boom! Boom!

I staggered up from the floor where I was sprawled, nearly slipping on a pool of half dried vomit next to the sofa. I was a mess.

The knocking happened again, coming from the door. I could hear someone calling too. "Mr Smith, this is the hotel manager. Please open the door!"

The room spun as I made it to the door, blurring and then coming back together. I scrabbled at the lock for a minute, before I realised it was already unlocked. I pulled it open.

"Hello?", I said, feeling like a wounded animal.

"Mr Smith, we need you to settle your account".

"Okay, I, err?

"It will need to be a bank transfer. If you'll come down to the lobby we can take care of it for you".

"Wow, that... that sounds like a lot. How... how much do I owe you?"

The hotelier looked apologetic. "It is a large sum, sir. I'm afraid it's...", he looked at a piece of paper, "Four million, one hundred thousand dollars".

What little colour I had left me then, along with another belly-load of vomit.

The rest of my trip was a hellish blur. The police were involved, when it was clear I actually didn't quite have enough money to cover my debt, even after I converted every last penny to US currency. In the end they let me off the last $10,000 as a sign of "goodwill".

My return to the airport was ignominious. No limo this time: I was in the back of a police cruiser.

The next few years were absolute rock bottom for me. Every moment, every opportunity, every friendship; all expended in the hunt to win back the unwinnable. Lost absolutely *everything*.

But now I'm here. I know who I am, and I know my problem. In a way I'm actually in a great place. Don't get me wrong - three million quid would improve things no end, but I'm satisfied with my lot right now.

It's not the same thrill I used to chase, but I'm hunting down a slower, quieter sort of victory. Every day I'm doing it. Not winning against luck, but winning against the brokenness inside of me.

You know what? In a way, it's the greatest high I've ever experienced. I just wish it came with a gold bathtub too.

REVELATIONS IN THE SALOON CAR

Revelations in the Saloon Car

400 mystery surprise

The lights flickered, slightly, as the train carriage rattled over a connection.

"I expect you are wondering why I've called you all together", said Miss Howthy, her horn-rimmed spectacles framed by a perfectly pinned hair bun.

"Yer gonna tell us who done the murders, right?" drawled Devon. His lack of alibi and previous criminal record had made him the police's first suspect, but no incriminating evidence had been unearthed.

"Not so quick, Mr Briley", she admonished, raising a single finger, "That was not the only crime committed here."

Stammering, a thin gentleman with a dishevelled comb-over spoke up, "Is this about the insurance? Look, I didn't want to do it, but SHE...". He trailed off, pointing limply at a buxom lady in an emerald green dress.

She, the widow Catton, coughed exasperatedly, "Oh, what nonsense. Maybe I encouraged a little *exaggeration* in the paperwork - but that doesn't make me a *murderer!*"

Reverend Dimble, a portly man in an unimaginative suit, spoke, "If I may, Miss Howthy, but I'm not clear why we should be listening to a retired schoolmistress? Surely this is a matter for the courts?"

"Clearly", said Miss Howthy, a glint of steel in her implacable hazel eyes, "each of you desires that this matter remain *firmly* outside of the public eye. Does anyone deny that?"

A guilty silence provided implicit confirmation.

"You, Mr Briley, didn't want any further investigation at the school, not if it might undercover your horticultural endeavours in *the boiler room*?" Devon hung his head in sullen defeat.

She turned to her right. "Mrs Catton, Mr Primp, you feared the scandal of your affair would leave you destitute. You aimed to elope and fund it with illicit gains". The two harrumphed but said nothing, unable to deny the plain truth.

She lay one hand on the rear carriage handle, as the vicar wilted under her stare, "What would the Church think, Reverend, of an attempt to conceal a death, even if the tower restoration fund *did* receive a generous donation?"

"I leave it to you all to do the right thing", she said. Even as the carriage exploded in recriminations behind her, the stern, measured woman had opened the door, and stepped on to the rear cargo platform.

She released the pin. Her freight wagon slowed and fell away from the train.

The rear carriage disappeared as she watched, carrying the culprits to their fate, and her to her own.

A. T. CROSS.
Stylographic Pen.

No. 232,804.   Patented Oct. 5, 1880.

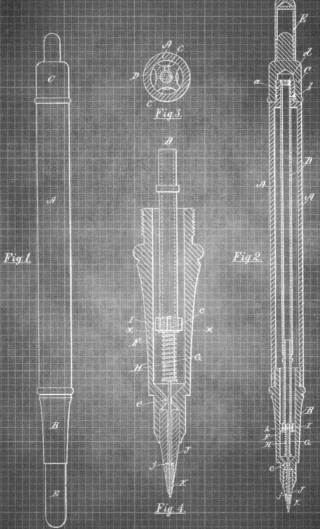

Fig.3.

Fig.1.

Fig.2.

Fig.4.

Witnesses.

Joseph A. Scholfield.
H. W. Hubbard.

Inventor.

Alonzo T. Cross.

Use of a discreet blotting sheet

200 historical technology

In my line of business, blotter paper is an unfortunate necessity. Since I lack the innate cleanliness of my higher born peers, ink stains are a perturbing regularity.

A clerk of my limited stature lacks the means to replace linen cuffs, and nor can I afford such an appearance that may cause my employees to demote me. My solution to dishevelment - and unemployment - is a discrete sheet of blotter paper on each sleeve, folded neatly over, so as to appear intrinsic to my dressing. This has the feature of protecting my most vulnerable clothing edge; cuffs being adjacent to the hands that hold the pen, fill the inkwell, *et cetera*; whilst also providing the facility to deftly remove any offending spillage before there can arise any detriment in my attire.

Of course, avoiding the whole enterprise would be preferable. I file, on occasion, for John J. Loud, a lawyer and self-styled 'Inventor'. He claims a patent of an improved writing implement, one with a ball at its point, at once preserving ink whilst neatly delivering it.

Sadly, I suspect this "ball point" is little more than whimsy, though I cannot deny that freedom from the blotter would be most welcome.

At that exact moment, Eloise tripped. A second later? She'd have lost her head. The screeching scumbag flew over her, so close she felt the wind in its spikes.

She leaned into the fall, rolling to the side. This was fortuitous too, since one of the thing's clawfists slammed into the soil where she had been laying an instant earlier.

Keeping moving was the only option. Clearly; staying still would have already killed her twice in three seconds.

There was a handrail mounted above a low wall. She sprinted to it, grabbing it, and leaping into the unknown.

Have you ever seen one of those parkour videos, where some insanely confident kid leapfrogs over stuff, and perfectly places their feet on the next obstacle - at least 20 feet away and impossibly far below. They convert human movement into a fluid.

Okay, now keep that image in mind. Got it? Think on it, as Eloise gets a foot caught under the rail, slamming her centre of balance way, way, *way* out of line. Remember that perfect, peerless parkour kid, as Eloise just falls, just straight down FALLS, headfirst, onto the concrete below.

The world went completely white for an instant, then her vision returned. It was coloured with red, thanks to the blood pouring from a gash on her scalp.

She was in no state to run, at this point. Her peripheral vision was being wrecked by the salty sticky warmth gushing out of her head. Desperately she wiped her eyes, and clambered into a half-bent shuffle.

She could make out a door. A door. Maybe the stalking terror wouldn't be able to manage door handles. She staggered faster, streams of gooey haemorrhage progressively blocking her view.

Somehow, she reached the doorway. A smeary red hand frantically tried the latch. Locked. She hammered it with a fist in frustration, leaving a messy red splodge.

The crunch of disturbed gravel told her that the monster had landed. Its fetid breath blew through her hair; so close. Her end was here.

She straightened. If this was to be her last stand, she'd face it head on.

As she steeled herself, the bloody stain shimmered in front of her. The entire door turned transparent, and a man in steel armour stepped out, marching past her!

"Jack?!", she whispered, her voice high pitched in shock.

She turned, and watched, as his blade flashed in the moonlight.

Unyielding bars. Row upon row; each cell the exact, monotonous same. Impassible lines, marking lives curtailed by retributive justice.

There was no thought given for the reasons a person was incarcerated. Humans might have cared, but to the system, each individual was a number.

Prisoner 78768 clasped the cold steel of his door, and squeezed. It felt the same as it had every morning since they'd arrived, and would do each one of the next seven hundred and twenty-six days.

Finally though, today, they acknowledged it. All of it. They were *here*, and it was time to stop wishing otherwise.

Red and green

Elmer tightened up the last screw. The silver of metal contrasted with the painted gloss of the frame, a shining indentation within a perfect sea of white.

He let the door swing loose now. The folded cardboard was no longer needed to support the weight of the door against the hinge, it kicked loose easily.

After several test closures, Elmer was satisfied; it was a neat fit. He put the dark grey screwdriver back into his lighter shaded tool bag, and zipped it up.

He took a glance around the room; with the fitting of the final cupboard, the job was finished, and the house was spick and span. Elmer was happy for the young couple, soon to move in. Carefully setting the latch, he gave the room a last nod of appreciation and let the front door close behind him.

It was getting near sunset now, the brightness of the sky at the horizon fading to a dirty grey overhead. He sighed. Try as he might, he couldn't stop his attention being drawn to the advertising board suspended above the road. A kaleidoscope of vibrant tones screamed out "Buy this! You need this! Look at me!". So much more insistent than the sky.

Elmer strolled along the street, his bag hanging loosely at his side. It was heavier every year; he remembered when he would carry every tool to every job. These days he'd leave his hammer at home if he could.

There were oak trees along the avenue, broad grey stretches of leaves, the chlorophyll making them so dark they seemed almost black in the twilight.

He picked up a leaf and held it. It was striking against his liver spotted hands. Grey and grey, yes, but subtly different, all the same.

Still, it wasn't right, certainly. Grey trees. And grass, that took a lot of life out of things. He looked at the little park nearby; a bite-sized paradise, suppressed by its monochromaticity. Even there, out of the corner of his vision, the reflection of a TV, across the square. There was green there, for the purpose of selling a carpet, as far as he could see.

The decision to remove colour from the world had not been taken lightly. Elmer didn't know the specifics, something to do with carbon-capture and a climate rescuing atmospheric filter on sunlight. It had saved the world, but the penalty had been absolute. Colour, gone.

Of course, workarounds had been found. "Quantum Light", whatever that meant, or growing things outside of the atmosphere. Both were expensive. And an old man looking at trees wasn't worth real money, not like carpet commercials, apparently.

Elmer strolled on. A smaller park, on his right, filled with children running and playing. They didn't know what they were missing, and that probably made it better. He tilted his head at their happy laughter.

At the bottom of the road lay the crossroads. Right was home. He usually went that way, but sometimes he went left. If the mood took him. Today it had.

Soon enough, he pushed the door open to the shop, and smiled. The nice lady behind the counter smiled back. "Back again?", she said.

"I think I need another one", he explained.

She nodded, and put on a pair of gloves. "What takes your fancy today?"

He already knew the answer, "Anything green".

He left the store, holding his purchase. It was wrapped in a layer of paper. A single rose, lipstick red, with luscious, almost velvet foliage.

He walked home. On the way, he didn't notice anything else at all.

Just red and green.

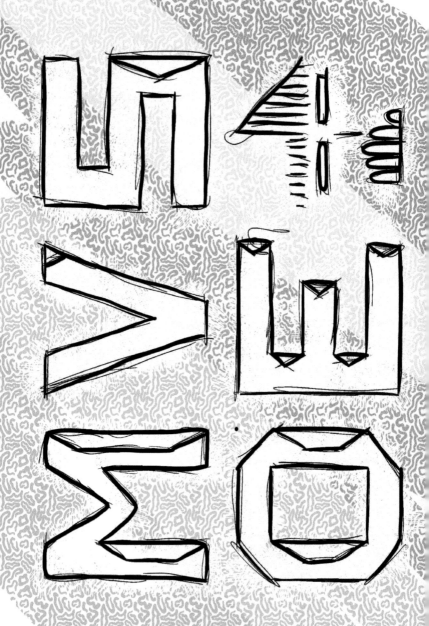

Moves

100 discopunk betrayal

The bodies on the dancefloor undulated to the laserpop beat, like a glass of water on top of a washing machine.

Arna stood, the only person unmoving. She was hacked off. That zarking move-stealer Annak!

As she threaded through the crowd, the houselights began to flicker, a staccato siren to warn of the upcoming competition. Arna's heart sank. Despite herself, her gaze shifted to the highest dance platform, now highlighted by hundreds of lasers.

Even amidst the flesh multitudes, pumping tuneage and insane lighting, she could see her rival's silhouette.

It was the dance-off final; and Annak was fighting dirty.

Beans. It's weird, the things you miss. Stringy old runner beans. I never even ate mine as a child - "Too chewy mummy, I don't want them!" But now there's whole days where I crave the texture of them; the strands stuck between my teeth.

Even so, there's no point in pining, because I can't have them. There aren't any runner beans on the station. On any station. Shame, when you consider that early NASA researchers even grew them on the ISS. That was when we had the luxury of time for science rather than survival.

After the Impact, every single jot of thought, money and rocket fuel went to getting as many people off-planet as possible. No time for scientists. In the broken dishwasher of bureaucracy that ensued, some administrator in charge of "What to Eat?" decided that those particular climbing beans would get too confused without gravity, so they didn't pack any.

And then the Earth died.

There might be some beans we could use down there, but between the supervolcanoes and acid monsoons, it's a pretty slim chance. I'm not going down looking, anyway.

So there's no beans for dinner. There will never be, ever again, for anyone. I mean, apart from kidney beans. And soya.

And... lima, is it? And all the others. Look, yes, there will be lots of *beans* for dinner. Too many, and too often, frankly. But those lovely stringy runners, in their little jackets you can pop open with your tongue, and then crunch beneath your teeth? Never again.

No, baked beans are *not* just as good! Are you serious? I miss the organic connection to something real, something unprocessed, something Earthly. Not aching *baked beans*! They're just sugar and tomato paste.

Look, you never had runner beans, you... you won't understand. I just miss 'em, that's all.

Commuting is the worst

600 cyperpunk urban

Shimmering towers punctured the horizon. Each was splashed with precise, geometric stripes of neon. The effect was jarring, brightest bright against darkest dark; enough to temporarily disrupt your vision if you looked directly. It made it hard to even tell the nevernet was active, the tiny pinpoints of its perimeter across the sky hidden by the distant misty glow of the arcologies. Of course, the nevernet *was* active, or they'd all be dead, especially at this time in the chitters' breeding season.

Rez sniffed the air, using xis olfactory senses to provide the information that overwhelmed retinas had failed to. The acrid tang of billions of vaporised bugs was in the air. The nevernet was doing its job.

Xe sighed, flaps wide. If you've never seen a zylac sigh, it's a recognisably similar action to a human exhalation, except - given the lack of a mouth - zylacs have wide resp flaps that swing to either side of xir faces as air is released. Frightening to the uninitiated human, but entirely benign.

Rez flicked on xis hud unit, seeing if there was any update to numerous job postings. Nada. Xe rolled xis eyes. It was the programmed command for turning off the hud visuals, but on this occasion it also summed up xis reaction to a disappointingly empty inbox.

A buzzing flared through the lobby; the pod had docked. With slumped shoulders, Rez joined the queue of other dispirited travellers, and squeezed into the grubby interior. No one took the pods if they could afford to avoid them. As the doors closed, Rez tried to ignore the odour filling the space; the reek of over-worked civs and resent.

The pod detached. A gentle vibration filled the cabin, a sign that the gravpump was barely functioning. Rez gripped a handhold and gritted xis teeth. The pods were funded by industry taxes; their job was to get civs from residences to work and back. Keeping them comfortable was not particularly relevant to this task. More than once Rez had been on a pod when the gravpump had failed. Spent the rest of the journey pinned to the back wall by g-force, barely able to breath from the pressure. No one took pods if they could afford to avoid them.

Some nights Rez would use the journey to watch a sim on xis hud, or catch up on some reading. Tonight though, xe felt too low for any of that. It was easier to gaze at the blaring horizon and feel miserable.

"Long shift comin' up?", a voice intruded.

Alongside sighing, another physiological challenge zylacs face is an anatomical inability to hide irritation: xir eyes flash orange when disturbed. Rez tried to keep them closed, but it was pointless.

The speaker was clearly alarmed, "No, no, rude of me to ask, sorry..."

"Look, I'm not annoyed with you, it's the job", Rez said.

Boredom apparently overcame the speaker's fear. "What... what do you do?"

Rez's flaps flew wide again, as xe gave another involuntary sigh. The whole cabin was noticeably brighter now, with the light emitted from the zylac's irisvents. Other civs had noticed, and were backing up - as much as that was possible in the limited space. The only thing Rez hated more than xis job was the reaction of other people.

"I work for the hivers". The speakers eyes widened in shock.

At that moment, the gravpump failed with a 'clunk', and the entire mass of civs were thrown to the back of the speeding pod. Humans and Xenos rammed together helplessly.

The cabin burned in the light of an enraged, orange glow.

The perfect preserve

She always gets it perfectly right. Never too much, never too little. "A perfect jam-to-dough ratio", the judges say. And that's not forgetting the jam itself. Not too sweet, not too tart; "a perfect preserve".

And so, every year, she wins. First place. Leaving the pickings for the rest of us. "Oh well done Doris, second place". She can stick it where the jam don't shine.

I wasn't having it this year, nope, not again. Only took an hour in her pantry, emptying out her special jars, and adding an extra little something.

We'll see whose doughnuts are "too sweet" now, won't we?

"Fair cop, you've got me!"

"Put your hands up!", the guard snarled.

"Err... are you sure?"

"Just do it".

I put my hands up. Or down. It's quite hard to define really, when you are flipped, and hanging off a rope. With my arms outstretched I could nearly touch the floor.

"What are you doing in here?", he asked.

"Well. That's a complicated question. Let me start at the beginning..."

We never really noticed money being privatised. If you'd asked someone, "Who prints banknotes?", they might have said it was the Bank of England, or America, or Sweden. Wherever. But would they have been *absolutely* sure it wasn't outsourced to some commercial company?

After the Covid-19 crisis, lots of changes happened, remote working, hands-off operations. It was already happening, but that sped things up. Without the average citizen being aware of it, credit card companies, banks, they all started to merge. Collude. Monopolise.

Look, money isn't real, is it? It's just this collective lie that a thing is worth a thing. We used to barter. You know, I'll give you this goat, you give me that bread. Now we just say that five units of currency is worth the same as a goat and use that instead. I mean, I think goats probably cost more than that, that's not the point. Money isn't real, that's what I'm saying. And if money isn't real, then electronic money is even less real. Just some ephemeral concept. 1s and 0s. And that makes it very easy for someone else to control.

When it happened, everyone was replaced. Individuals, companies, governments. One world order, "Powered by Vista". The thing is, capitalism only works when the collective lie is intact: "Money equals freedom". Without some hint of freedom, the veil is torn away, and you are slaves to a system.

A system, in this case, that held literally all the cards. Want to riot? Guess who pays the police? Guess who owns the law, for that matter. Vista didn't pretend to be anything except what it was: a private club, for the exclusive benefit of the 0.001%. The rest of us 99.999%? Just fuel for the machine.

"That's treason, that it", the guard said. Just firmly enough that the cameras would record it. He didn't stop me though.

I wasn't even born when this all happened. The only life I've known is this one; servitude. Not even sure what I'm serving, I just know that Vista pulls the strings on *everything*. There was this one time, back in educamp. I must have been, what, eight? I'd found some paper and a pencil, and I'd drawn a lovely little picture of the sky. There were trees, a little round sun. A teacher found it, and the look on her face. "You've stolen these! Vista provides these materials for education. I'll have to report this waste."

Eight years old. I should have been playing with cuddly toys, or kicking a ball around. Instead I was being guilt-groomed to play my part in a system that didn't care about me in the slightest.

Eight years old.

"It's part of everyone's training; can't have everyone going around wasting time and resources". He said it, the guard, but there was a gleam in his eyes, never-the-less. I think he was thinking about his own constrained childhood. All of our wasted years.

I think that's where it started. The sense that all this, *all of it*, is wrong. I didn't do anything about that day, except crying, but I've never forgotten. And when I hit my teens and started in the worklines, well, I kept my eyes open.

You might not realise it, but there's a hidden world out there. Underneath the sheen of pretence, there's a normal existence possible beneath it. I'm not going to tell you the details, not in here, but I managed to join a cell of The Resist. And then... I left.

"What do you mean, you left?"

"I left. Look", I said. I waved my arm.

He took it, then turned it round hurriedly. He grabbed my other arm. "Where is it? You have no chip!".

"That's right dude!" I grinned, "Vista can't see me".

The flaw in a perfect system is that it knows it's perfect. It knows it's all encompassing, all controlling. Nothing can stop it.

That, of course, means it's overconfident. Can't conceive of a situation where it *isn't* perfect. If all citizens are assigned a number, forced into a role, if they all know their place, then what happens when they... don't? If there can't be a citizen without a number, without an ID, then there's no plan for when a citizen doesn't have one.

"What are you saying?", said the guard. He wasn't feigning interest now, he genuinely needed to know.

"I'm saying that I'm not here". I waved at the camera. "Those cameras automatically read you, and store footage with your chipnumber. If there's no chip, it discards the footage, because there is no citizen involved. It can't see me".

The guard stared at the camera, and then raised an eyebrow at me, "Why are you here?".

An explosion detonated, far off on the other side of the facility. "That's the first data bank. Right now, The Resist is blowing the backups. Worldwide". I spun upright, and released my harness.

I pointed at the camera, "They can't see any of us now".

Thoughts from the author

I'll admit; with this project, I had very little idea what I was letting myself in for. I knew I could write *in general*, and I'd written a few pieces of microfiction as preparation, but this was different. I was jumping into the deep end - with judges waiting!

Helpfully, I've always been a pantser rather than a plotter, so having a sudden list of stories generated for me was actually the only writing prompt I needed. I mostly just threw myself in headlong, started writing, and found a story developing - often somewhat to my surprise - as I went along. It was honestly a little bewildering; with each piece I found myself in thankful wonder at how a story had neatly uncurled into exactly the right space.

There *was* some aggressive editing needed - I've learnt that taking 20 words out of a 700 word piece is much more manageable than taking it out of 200 - but on the whole, you are so focused on precision during the process that you find yourself with surprisingly polished pieces at the end.

Now, there are obvious obstacles in microfiction: the chief being is that the pieces are super short. Obviously. As a result there's never enough room to unpack characters; you have to give them flavour as soon as possible. The same with storyline; I actually found middle length pieces the hardest;

500 words is more than a snapshot, but still too tiny to fit in a we-learnt-it-in-primary-school beginning, middle and end.

All-in-all, I'm very satisfied with how it all turned out, both the writing and the illustration, and the neat package they've become together. I hope you have found it as enjoyable to hold as I found producing it.

If you found the idea enticing, there's a do-it-yourself cheat sheet on page 172. I would *love* to read any microfiction you write as a result of this project - please send it to me through twitter @cmlowryauthor or the contact page on my website *http://www.allaboutchris.org.*

Finally, I found I had a strong temptation to drop in a surprise twists at the end of most sections. I'm sorry about that. I resisted, for the most part. Or did I?*

* I didn't

Favourite moments
introspection waffle

The hardest thing about writing microfiction is saying goodbye. As an author, all stories are your children. You wonder how they will grow up, what shape they will take after they leave your care.

With this project, that feeling is compounded; its not a single novel - I'm now left with thirty-three beginnings! Not to forget over a hundred characters, each of whom I want to follow, just to find out what happens next in their lives...

At the point of writing this ending it became clear that I actually had something to say about every story, so I thought I would. Apologies if that seems unbearably self-indulgent. It is. Probably crass and un-artistic too, especially in a book focused on conciseness.

You can always choose not to read any of the following; imagine I sagely preserved a veil of mystery instead.

Just the Sky

This steampunk story was one of the first pieces I wrote for the book. I was happy to manage to get so many 'mini' scenes into it, and introduce so many characters in just 700 words. Mouse (*they/them*) is possibly my favourite character in the whole book. If you liked this, I'd recommend the *Free Wrench* series by Joseph R Lallo, a lovely fistful of plucky adventurers in airships.

The Grand Service

I planned to make this story about *The Crown Jewels*, but some googling revealed the existence of *The Grand Service* so I changed tack. Interestingly, you really can put St James Palace into an energy switching website - in doing so, I did worry about being added to some kind of Government watch list. I don't think there is a print shop on Wanstead High Street though. Sorry.

Document OL1

I quite like the idea of ray diving. I think it reminds me of terrible films like "The Core", mixed with a bit of Red Dwarf - which, if you've not read, you should absolutely pick up the three Grant Naylor novels. Incidentally, a 'decant' was my name for a sort of metric 10 day space-week, did that work?

Wait

Writing in second person is hard! It was enjoyable to do it once, but it was only this and Open Drawers where I ran the risk. Both featuring challenging personal decisions, I now realise. And no, I don't know what you are agreeing to.

S.I.L.O.

"If the wilderness has no owner, then neither do I". It's not a quote from anywhere, as far as I can tell, but it sounds like it should be. If you love wild spaces, reading a little about the history of the Kinder Scout Mass Trespass is well worth it. If you want to get a little bit angry, a little bit revolutionary at the same time, I'd recommend The Book Of Trespass by Nick Hayes.

Eminently experimental

As an old stick-in-the-mud, I can get on board with coalpunk as a concept, even if it would be horribly labour intensive and smoky. I tried to get some authenticity to the concept of a coal charged battery, and the transient wet-cell is a concept from the very earliest of Victorian batteries. The locations try to be as true to reality as possible, having traced the route from the Barts 1870 map of Manchester. I did far, far too much reading into the history of the County Cricket Club as research. Approximately 0.1% of that reading made its way into the story: the name "Manchester Cricket Club".

Can't sail a hurricane

I was hesitant, attempting to add any kind of Southern US accent to a story; both out of fear of cultural appropriation, and of failure. I think I struck a decently flavoured-without-specificity approach here, also taking into account that the lingo would have been a bit different in the 1700s than now. Thanks to my Dad for casting an eye over the sailing terminology for me, and for the internet for the ludicrous amount of reading I did about mast numbers, ship speed and the advancements in sailing technology between 1600 and 1900. All for a 300 word story: I'm an easily distracted moron.

Open drawers

This story was mostly inspired by the recent house purchase we made, and the continuous irritation such a process provides through *estate agents*. The rest of the idea expanded from there. The question is, where would you land, if it was your house? I'm a Christian vegetarian pacifist and I'm still not sure what I would do!

Awake

I wrote this one in my head during a long bike ride on Anglesey. I mostly blame reading lots of the MÖRK BORG black-comedy horror role play game during that holiday.

Zero

As will be of no surprise if you've read this far, I did *a lot* of reading about anti-matter whilst writing this piece. Ultimately, I prefer to write hard sci-fi, being as accurate and realistic as possible, whilst also being free to flex the *fi* side of things too. So whilst an Exclusion Drive remains vague hypothetical nonsense, it has just enough flavour of something that *could* be real, if future understanding and reality of the universe happens to unfold in that direction.

Also, I really want to watch ZeroG Basketball.

Daily bread

Doing very little preparation or planning means that my inspiration has been hugely shaped by the things around me. I was wild camping, or about to embark on some anyway, when I began this story. I think I was slightly annoyed with the modern world too, and daydreaming about simply stealing the bits I needed from it and running away. Suze committed my crimes for me.

The wheels of progress

An email from work *definitely* played a part in this piece. The hallmarks of institutional idiocy should be familiar to anyone who has worked for a large organisation. Last summer, for example, on a boiling hot day at work, a nurse handed me an ice cream, "The kitchens have sent these down for us". I managed about one lick before a manager turned up and told us we weren't allowed to eat them until our breaks. My break wasn't for 3 hours, and I didn't have a freezer. "Errrk!"

"It doesn't matter"

I set myself the goal of an entire story in dialogue, with absolutely no descriptors or sentences outside of the contents of speech marks. It was much easier than I expected. JD Salinger wrote a short story called "Pretty Mouth and Green my Eyes" which didn't quite do this, but carried a huge amount of the storytelling in dialogue, and has stuck in my head for a decade.

All for the prize

Working for the NHS can feel like a slog sometimes, and I have had the (dis)pleasure of working for some A-grade narcissists, so there's elements of this to my own life. That said, I'm reasonably sure I've never poisoned a colleague's work so as to save the life of a supervisor. Might put that in my next appraisal...

Leaving nothing

Nanopunk is one of the many *somethingpunk* genres I had fun with, writing this book. This story was written whilst putting the book together, when I realised I'd accidentally written two 900 *crime hope* stories and missed a 600 crime hope. I let The Die Decide a new theme and category, and so we ended up with this story. Frankly, whilst I am excited about the potential advancements technology is going to bring us, I do think there's at least an 80% chance we are going to accidentally destroy the world. Shout out to the episode of Red Dwarf "Nanarchy", where Krypton gives a cloud of nanobots 'a good talking to' and so they overcompensate, building Lister a ridiculously uber-muscley new arm. Good times.

How it begins

Biopunk! There really are a million sub-genres within *nonsensepunk*! In a piece where I tried to embrace thematic cliché as much as possible, I also decided to add in the challenge of two non-binary characters. I often find writing prose with *they/them* characters a little more clunky and wordy, but I managed two characters with *they/them* and *it/it* in 100 words; like everything else, getting pronouns right just takes dedication and practice. The monster is named in dedication to seminal pulp-action author Clive Cussler, *King of Cliché*, sadly departed from us in 2020.

Leverö Öperk Moritus

Along with historical betrayal, the theme from this piece came from a conversation my brother Nick and I had during the summer: why is there hardly any medieval dystopia around? The 'ancient promise' is in a made-up language, broadly made from a mix of Swedish and Latin words. I, of course, had been reading far too much MÖRK BORG again when I wrote this. You can very much tell.

A new kind of politics

Gosh. This one is written in honour of the current Conservative government. Throw in a comment on social media echo-chambers and a deep disenfranchisement with the state of the modern world, and you've perfectly recreated the frame of mind that birthed this story.

Just as planned

There's a James Bond film with a machine gun filled chase on skis, right? Or is it *True Lies* with Arnold Schwarzenegger? There must be three or four Steven Seagal movies like that. This is for that one. All of them. Any of them.

Uqalekisiwe

Cultural appropriation is nasty, and I did my best to be respectful here. Thanks to the Port Nolloth community facebook group for your feedback and insights on the town, and a massive shout out to my Xhosa friend Zama for her input on slang terms, language use, and, of course, why no self respecting person would eat Cheetos when they could have amaNikNaks!

Community development

Lots of my church and volunteer work has involved a walking-through-treacle involvement with community centres, councils and interminable planning departments. I took some gentle creative liberties with the structure of prefabricated buildings here, but I suspect the broad idea *could* happen. The potential of bluffing one's way through red tape is definitely a fair reflection of reality.

The Perfect Crime

This is the piece I think would be most easily made into a film. I'm thinking a younger Jack Nicholson, smiling sardonically, following by a gritty flashback to some kind of bank-job-gone-wrong. Tell me it wouldn't make a killing at the box office. Also, I wrote this up at Burnmoor Lodge, in the Western Lake District, by gas lantern; the photo on page 150 was taken as I scribbled it on paper.

Solid gold

In an apt position, following the previous setting, I was tempted to write a story about a casino-job-gone-wrong, perhaps with a Lock Stock style cliffhanger. I struggled to find inspiration, mostly because in creative circles the cliched thing to do at a casino is to rob it. Less well explored, it seems to me, is the far more commonly trod path; foolishly losing everything.

Revelations in the Saloon Car

Cards on the table: I've never read an Agatha Christie novel. I pretty much just know of the whodunnit genre through its resonation in popular culture, referenced through Simpsons episodes and Radio 4 sitcoms. I did steal a decent amount of flavour from Clive Cussler's "Isaac Bell" series, most of which are set on trains at the turn of the last century.

Use of a discreet blotting sheet

John J. Loud actually invented the ballpoint pen about 20 years before the infamous László Bíró (as in, "anyone got a biro I can use?") did, but never managed to bring it to market. The picture here is made from the actual US patent application. I found myself in the mid 1800s in a number of these stories; I found it oddly enjoyable, although I do worry that I unwittingly bring linguistic and cultural anachronisms along for the ride. My deepest regrets to any Victorians reading.

Close

This was my snapshot of what real life experience in a 1st person computer game shooter would be. Doom, Quake, something like that. Co-op mode kicks in during the last 3 paragraphs.

78768

Last Friday, the total prison population of the UK was 78,768 people. More than 1 in 1000 of us are currently being deprived of our liberty. I suspect most of us would even agree with most of the sentencing, but we should all worry how much of it we would strongly *disagree* with.

Ashley Asti, in I have Waited For You: Letters from Prison, said *"So seamlessly have we (those in power) written over stories and lives like yours that, to someone like me, it is very easy not to hear about lives like yours. Not to know or imagine they exist. Not to know that public policy is failing you. Not to know that the prison system is an impoverished and wholly inadequate response to your experience and that it, too, is failing you. Which means it's failing all of us".*

Red and green

On my route home from work, they've just finished putting up another one of those vast electronic advertising boards, the 20 foot television screens designed to steal my attention and open my wallet. I'm not a fan. In fact, I think it should be criminalised. Wired Magazine wrote an article on it a few years ago. "Companies seize our time and attention for absolutely nothing in exchange, and indeed, without consent at all. This isn't just an annoyance. It's stealing". This piece extends that to the idea that even the very colours that we see could be held captive. Apologies to anyone sight impaired or colour-blind, no disrespect was meant, just an acknowledgement that the contents of our senses are precious.

Moves

As you've seen, I had many suggestions of different types of "punk" - cyberpunk, dieselpunk, etc - so when I was given the freedom of an entire punk category, I enjoyed exploring it...

...but the idea of a discopunk universe horrifies me.

Without gravity

Yes, I did a deep dive into plant growing on the International Space Station. NASA has a whole page on plants in space. Turns out gravity doesn't play as much of a role as you might think. Humanity has also grown plants on the moon, through the Chang'e-4 mission which left a heated, sealed Lunar Micro Ecosystem with fly eggs and seeds on the surface! For a sci-fi nerd, this stuff is so exciting, especially when it's as near as the Moon! Only 240,000 miles away - my Renault Scenic could drive that in 142 days! Admittedly, some slight adjustments might need to be made to it, but that's interesting too... *Runs off to write down idea for hard science story about converting an unreliable French automobile for atmospheric exit*

Commuting is the worst

Can we just agree on this one? Commuting *is* the worst. Unpaid time so you can get to the place where you trade even more of your rare life moments for drudgery. I made the effort to use a different set of pronouns here, Rez being an alien, and the setting using *xe/xis/xem* terms for xenos types. However, I'm also very aware some humans use these terms,

so it doesn't hurt for us all to become more familiar with
them.

The perfect preserve

I'm aware that two thirds of the stories featuring cooking
involve attempts at poisoning, but I'm not going to apologise.
My home town has annual competitive food shows, and I'm
surprised something like this hasn't happened already.

Invisible

I wrote this story by accident, getting confused and
repeating the 900 crime hope entry. That's fine though,
ended with a hopeful nod to the future, rather than the
suburban bake-off premeditations we'd have finished with
otherwise.

Artist credits

This project has been a lovely opportunity to work with some great artists, as well as get in touch with my own artistic skills, such as they are.

Below are the artists involved, the images they provided, and contact details if they are available for commission.

CM Lowry (me!)

Intro, Operation Instructions Series AB-96 Rayship, Wait, Can't sail a hurricane, Zero, "It doesn't matter", All for the prize, Leaving Nothing, How it begins, Leverö Öperk Moritus, A new kind of politics, Uqalekisiwe, Solid gold, Revelations in the Saloon Car, Use of a discreet blotting sheet, Close, Moves, The perfect preserve, Thoughts from the author.

Dave Emmerson

The Grand Service, S.I.L.O., Open drawers (*with help from Elijah Emmerson*), Daily Bread, Community development, 78768, Red and green - you can find more of Dave's innovative work and zines at visionspress.bandcamp.com.

Toby Prest
Just the Sky, Wheels of Progress, Commuting is the worst.

Gaelen Adric Izatt-Galloway III
Just as planned & Invisible - *find them @KillurMonkeyArt.*

Dickkie Watson
Without gravity & Finished - find them *@dickkie85.*

Wiley Murder Willis
Awake.

Joen Lowry
Wheels of Progress.

Free Use
Thanks to Ye Jinghan on Unsplash for image on 78768, Freepik.com for *High angle of woman feet in the sand* on Uqalekisiwe and Arthur Lien for image on The Perfect Crime, (*Chemerinsky during Hyatt III sketch* from Wikimedia Commons, Creative Commons Attribution-ShareAlike 4.0).
Cover Title Font: Arbutus Slab by Karolina Lach.
Content Font: Zilla Slab by The Mozilla Foundation

Let The Die Decide for you

Writing microfiction is a treat. I hope that this book has inspired you, dear reader, to consider making a stab at culturing your own cute shards of story.

To create your own writing prompts, using the same category and theme prompts that I did, simple roll a ten sided die 3 times on the table below. Have fun!

(*You can also visit* allaboutchris.org/microfiction *for a magic automated one.*)

Result	Length	Categories	Theme
1	100 words	Horror	Hope
2	200 words	Science Fiction	Betrayal
3	300 words	Crime	Surprise
4	400 words	Mystery	Survival
5	500 words	Historical	Acceptance
6	600 words	Punk	Dinner Time
7	700 words	Drama	Green Leaves
8	800 words	Outdoors	Technology
9	900 words	Casino	Urban
10	1000 words	Cookery	Mastery

Thank you, and good night!

It's over. Why are you still here? Go home!

There we go. All finished. Thank you so much for taking the time to read this, to support me on Kickstarter, to visit a friendly local bookshop, any of those things and more. I'm indebted to you, both for your belief in me, and the firm-prod-with-a-pointy-stick that knowing people were waiting had on my attitude to deadlines.

So yes, thanks. Please check out *@cmlowryauthor* on Twitter, Facebook and Instagram, and find other musings at my personal site: *allaboutchris.org*.

Thank you again, and bye!

What? Why are you still here?

You want one more story.

You know I already gave you nearly forty, right?

Noise of exasperated author sighing

You still want more? Okay, okay...

Come on Die, how long do I have?

noise of die rolling

4!

I have 40 words, to tell you a story? *Fine.*

I'll do it, and then it's over. See you all soon!

Finished

40 release barefoot

The initial joy of release, words escaping his fingers, had become heavier.

It was finished now, thankfully.

He focused, as he'd been taught. The weight grew less.

Carefully, he removed his footwear, opened the window, and soared into the sky.